WAGON TRAIN WEDDING

LINDA FORD

1

Santa Fe Trail, late fall, 1848

"What do you mean she's missing?" Gil Trapper, scout for the Santa Fe Trail wagon train looked at the worried faces around him. How could Judith Russell be missing? She'd been traveling with the train since they left Independence near on to a month ago. From the beginning she'd been a good traveler, doing her share, and helping others. His observations said she was not the sort to do something foolish. He tried to think what else he knew of her. Sister to seasoned traders on the trail, Luke and Warren. Younger than either of them. Seems he'd heard Luke say she was twenty. Not that her age had any bearing on this situation.

"She was out walking by the wagons. We didn't think much at first when she wasn't here when we stopped. We thought maybe she'd fallen behind and would catch up. But she should have been here by now and she isn't. And we don't see her coming." As she talked, Luke's wife, Donna Grace, clutched her infant to her breast as if afraid the baby girl would up and disappear.

The others joined in, voicing their concerns.

Before Gil could reassure them that she had simply fallen behind, Luke and Warren rode up on horseback.

"We're going to find our sister," Warren said.

Gil nodded. "Let me inform Buck and I'll join you in searching." As the wagon master, Buck needed to know what was going on. "The rest of you stay here and take care of things."

Having noticed the worried knot of people, Buck rode up, demanded and received an explanation. He didn't offer any empty consolations. They were all aware of how many disasters could have befallen the woman.

"We'll ride along the back trail," Warren said.

Gil accompanied the brothers. After two miles with no sight of her, they reined up to consider what to do.

"You two stick to the trail," Gil said. "If she's simply fallen behind, she'll know enough to stay on it." Or if she'd been injured in a fall or—there were hundreds of reason she might not be able to catch up. "I'll ride toward the river and search there. Not that I expect to find anything."

They parted ways and Gil turned off the trail.

Every nerve in his body twitched with tension. If she'd simply fallen behind, they should have come upon her by now. Unless she'd gotten turned around and lost her way. Or had been set upon by one or more of those preying upon the wagon trains.

He guided his mount toward the bushes and trees along the river, pausing often to listen for any sound. Crows squawked at his intrusion. Smaller birds rustled in the autumn dried leaves. Coyotes began their mournful cry. His skin prickled with the knowledge that wolves had been spotted a day ago.

He rode onward, looking for any sign, listening for any sound. It would soon be dark. *Lord, help us find her.*

He jerked forward and strained toward the faint sound of a... baby crying? Surely he was mistaken. It must be some wild animal, though he couldn't think what one made that sound.

Edging his horse toward the sound, he picked a path that allowed him to move quietly. He stuck his handgun into his belt and pulled his rifle from the scabbard.

A flash of movement caught his eye. He reined in and slowly dismounted, easing forward with the skill that four years on the trail had taught him until he had a clearer view.

"Judith," he murmured.

She turned. "Thank goodness. I am thoroughly lost and so is this little one." She tipped her head toward a girl child in her arms.

"Where did you find that?"

At his voice, the child looked at him with wide blue eyes. Her tousled hair was the color of liquid sunshine. She stuck two fingers in her mouth and sucked noisily.

He squatted down five feet from the pair, knowing he would be less scary to the girl if he wasn't towering over her.

"I heard her crying, though at the time I was simply curious as to what it was. I know she must have parents somewhere but I've looked and looked. That's how I became so disorientated and lost sight of the wagons." She glanced past him. "How far are we from them?"

"Five miles more or less." He pushed to his feet. "I best find her parents." But as he headed back to his horse, Judith hurried after him.

"I'm going with you."

He considered his options. If he took them with him it would slow him down but he would know they were safe and wouldn't have to back track. "Come along." Upon his return to the horse, he reached for the child.

Judith hesitated before she released her hold.

Gil took a good look at the little one who returned his study, her lips quivering. "She's just a baby."

"Old enough to walk. I think she must have wandered away. Her parents will be beside themselves with worry."

Gil helped Judith to the saddle with one hand then lifted the little girl to her. Leading the horse, he slowly made his way through the bushes, looking for any sign of the parents.

"Where would she have come from?" Judith's voice revealed a good deal of worry and a hefty dose of fatigue. She must have wandered about for several hours, anxious to reunite the baby with the doubtlessly worried parents.

"There's a wagon train a few days ahead of us. They left a month before us." What sort of delays had caused them to lose so much time? "One of the wagons must had dropped out." He could think of no other explanation for a baby out in the wilds.

They continued for the better part of an hour, his attention on the ground. He often stopped and studied his surroundings. Something caught his attention and he bent low to the ground. "Wagon tracks." They were several days old but no mistaking them and they went straight toward a thicket of trees. "You better stay here while I have a look."

She looked ready to argue until she looked at the child in front of her. "I'll wait here." She'd correctly read his concern about what he might discover.

He led the horse to the protection of some trees against a rocky bank.

"If you hear gunshots, ride up the hill. You'll come to the dusty trail in about a mile. Turn right and keep going."

"And leave you? That doesn't seem correct."

"You can send back Buck or your brothers. But you must protect the child."

Judith's brown eyes held his, direct, challenging. He'd noted this about her already. A woman who wouldn't back away from a challenge and who made it clear she didn't expect to sit back and let others take care of her.

He waited for her cooperation.

Only after she nodded did he cradle his rifle in his arms and on silent feet, make his careful way toward the trees and whatever he might find there.

The bushes and branches were battered by people passing through. A few more feet and he saw a wagon tipped over, contents scattered wildly. He remained in the trees, watching for signs of danger. A groan drew his attention and he slipped through the trees to the other side of the clearing.

His heart gave a violent beat at the sight of a man and woman on the ground, their clothes blood soaked. A glance informed him the woman was dead. He passed her and fell to his knees by the man. The color had left his face. Gil knew he watched the life leaving him.

"What happened?" Gil asked.

"Left wagon train. Wife sick. Robbers came upon us. Baby?" He tried to sit up.

Gil eased him back. "We found your daughter. She's safe."

"Thank God." The man shuddered. "She's Anna Harris. Anna. Eighteen months old." He grabbed the front of Gil's shirt. "Take her. Raise her as your own. We have no family."

"She'll be well taken care of. I can assure you of that."

Mr. Harris's grip tightened, his strength surprising considering his condition. "Promise me *you* will raise her."

How could he? He wasn't even married. Had no intention of entering that state. Oh sure. Once he'd thought it was what he wanted. Before Lillian had made him think otherwise. Finding her in the arms of another man when she talked of love and marriage to Gil had left him disillusioned about the faithfulness of a woman. He certainly had no notion of repeating his mistake.

Mr. Harris clutched at Gil's shirt, a look of determination on his face. "I won't let you go until you give me your word to take Anna."

Gil unhooked the man's fingers and eased him to the ground. "You have to understand I am not married. I can't raise her." Gil's insides shriveled as the man sobbed. "But I promise I will find a good family for her."

"Thank you." Mr. Harris closed his eyes and struggled for breath. "We've been robbed but if there is anything you can use..."

"I'll take care of everything. You sure there's no one I should notify?"

"Tell Anna how much we loved her." A inhalation shuddered in and out.

Gil watched Mr. Harris's chest. But he'd taken his

last breath. "Good bye. I'll make sure Anna knows she is loved."

He pushed to his feet and looked about. Torn clothing tossed about. Flour scattered recklessly. A trunk with the top torn asunder. Two bodies to take care of.

An hour later, with darkness closing in about him, he returned to Judith. Little Anna slept in her arms. He carried with him a bundle of clothing for the girl and a few items that had not been destroyed.

"What did you find?" Judith asked.

Gil could not say if it was fear or fatigue or even hunger that made her voice quiver. The darkness had deepened so he couldn't make out her features well enough to read her expression.

"You might as well get down while I tell you." He reached up for the sleeping Anna, holding her in one arm while he assisted Judith to the ground.

He led her to shelter by the trees. They sank to the grass and he told her what he had discovered. "I promised him I would see that the baby had a home."

"I'll keep her," Judith said. "She's quite won my heart. I'll love her and take care of her as if she was my own flesh and blood."

LITTLE ANNA'S head rested against Judith's shoulder. Earlier, Judith had given her water from her canteen and a biscuit from her pocket. The child had fallen asleep, exhausted from crying and wandering about lost. "I will keep her," she repeated, her voice growing stronger. From the moment she'd discovered little Anna, Judith's heart had opened up and embraced her. Warren's son had died five years ago. Judith's baby sister had slipped away when Judith was seven. She missed them both and it made her want to protect and cherish this child. Her desire was magnified by the acknowledgment that she would not marry and have a child of her own. Her heart had been broken by the death of Frank, her fiancé. She'd had quite enough of loving and losing in her life.

She ignored the possibility of more loss in her own future if she opened her heart to a child that could be snatched from her at any time. If not by someone claiming her then perhaps by illness or accident. Life was so uncertain. It made her want to shut herself off to risk but she couldn't deny the protectiveness she felt toward this child. Little Anna had lost her parents. Judith would make sure she knew nothing but love.

"You're unmarried. You have no home. How will you take care of her?"

The reasonableness of the man's question did nothing to make Judith change her mind.

"I'll manage somehow." She knew how difficult it was for a woman alone to raise a child and she had no plans for the future apart from finding the man she blamed for her fiancé's death and letting him know just how selfish his choices had been. Once she'd accomplished that she would find the ways and means of providing for herself and Anna. "Besides you're not married either and you are a scout on the Santa Fe Trail."

"I didn't say I'd keep her. I said I would find her a family."

Judith couldn't miss the way he emphasized the final word.

Before she could argue Gil pulled forward two small bundles. "I found some clothing and things for her. And I managed to rescue a bit of food. We should eat."

"Shouldn't we rejoin the others?" A single man and a single woman alone for the night. It compromised both of them.

"We'll stay here, and catch up to the wagon train in the morning." His voice gave no clue as to how he felt about the situation.

She wasn't prepared for the consequences of such an arrangement. "I'm not afraid to travel after dark. All we have to do is find the trail and stay on it."

"It would be too dangerous."

"I have no intention of spending the night alone with you." She made it to her feet. Anna whined at being disturbed.

"Have you considered that the men who robbed that wagon and murdered those people are still out there?"

She sat back down with a thud. "I have no wish to be accosted by such men."

"Seems wise to me."

"There's lots of wood here. We could build a fire." Hot food and warmth would do much to make her more comfortable. As soon as she spoke the words she knew they were foolish. "Never mind. I don't want to signal those awful men our whereabouts."

"Another wise decision."

Gil's calm acceptance of their situation made her even more resentful of it.

"I found some biscuits and cooked meat." He untied one bundle.

Anna wakened and reached for a biscuit. The three of them munched on the food. With darkness came the cold of the November night. Judith shivered and wished for her warm shawl or a woolen blanket. She pulled Anna into her arms to keep her warm.

"Mama," Anna demanded.

"Honey, you have to stay here with us. Cuddle up and I'll keep you warm."

Anna pushed away. "Mama." She squirmed from Judith's arms and toddled away.

Judith caught her. "It's too dark to look for your mama."

Anna squirmed and fussed but Judith would not let her go.

"Hush, baby," she crooned. "Go to sleep." She sang a lullaby she'd heard from her own mother.

Anna struggled a few more minutes than stuck her two fingers in her mouth and within minutes fell asleep.

Neither Judith nor Gil spoke. On her part, Judith

didn't want to disturb the sleeping baby. But she must get Gil's agreement on a certain matter.

"I really want to keep her. After all, I am the most familiar person she has left. It wouldn't be fair for her to have that snatched away as well."

"She hardly knows you better than anyone else after just a few hours."

Judith considered herself a rational person, not given to outbursts or foolish arguments but Gil's calm reasonableness caused something inside her to snap. "Where are you going to find a family for her? Most of those on the wagon train are rough drivers."

"There's your brother. He's married now."

"Luke and Donna Grace. Yes, but they have a new baby."

"What makes you think they wouldn't welcome an older child?"

Judith wished she could see the man, but it was too dark so she had to be content with what she knew of him. Dark brown eyes, brown hair. A strong jaw and a mobile mouth. Until now she had considered him both kind and steady, but now she saw his steadiness for what it truly was—stubbornness.

"What makes you think they would?" She sounded petulant and petty but she couldn't help it.

"I guess I'll ask them."

Was there a way she could speak to them first and ask them to say no? Judith could tell them that she had fallen in love with this child the minute she'd found her, weary and tearful and asking for her mama and papa. Something about the child's woefulness had touched a familiar chord in Judith's heart. She'd felt weary and tearful and abandoned when she'd learned of Frank's death. Still did, if truth was to be told.

She'd promised to help Anna find her parents.

Now, she silently promised, she'd give the child the love and attention her parents would have given.

All she had to do was convince Gil, with his quiet stubbornness, to let her keep Anna.

2

Gil took a swallow of water and passed the canteen to Judith. She swallowed twice and returned it to him. He capped it firmly. Hot coffee would have been a nice treat but he had no trouble accepting the necessity of keeping their whereabouts as secure as possible.

"She hasn't cried much," he observed.

"I think it means she trusts me."

"Could be." He'd said about all he meant to on the subject of Anna staying with Judith and hoped she would let it go.

"I think her trust should be honored." She said it with such conviction he wondered if she had more reason than little Anna for her statement. If he knew her better he might be tempted to ask. Would she tell him if he did? Perhaps someone had not honored her trust. He knew how that felt. He thought of Lillian and how she'd told him what she thought he wanted to hear. Or what served her best with no regard for the truth.

"It's going to be a cold night." Would she understand he didn't wish to talk about Anna's future? He'd vowed to find the child a family. Not a single woman. The only family on the wagon train was Luke and Donna Grace. Or the preacher and his wife but they were getting on in years.

He stared at the crescent moon. They were the only options until they reached one of the little stopping posts or Fort Mann. From what he'd seen of such places, the probability of finding the sort of family he had in mind was unlikely. Perhaps there existed a family on the wagon train ahead of them, one who had known the Harrises.

He didn't know how long he'd mused about his responsibility regarding the child until a sound drew his attention.

Was that Judith's teeth chattering?

"Are you cold?" The temperature had dropped. Indeed, he began to shiver. "I've got a blanket." He always carried one in case he had to spend the night out in the open. Often he did it without the comfort of a fire. But never before had he done it in the company of a woman and child.

He went to his horse where he had left it to graze, but saddled, should he need a quick getaway. He took out the narrow blanket and draped it around Judith's shoulders.

"Thanks," she said and drew it protectively about herself to shelter the baby.

He sat down again, close enough to share a hint of body heat, but not so close she would feel he was inappropriate. That's when it hit him like a kick from an angry mule.

They were alone together for the night. What would people say? Not that it mattered to him. He could simply ride away.

But Judith's reputation would be marred.

He shifted away.

"Aren't you cold?" she asked.

Cold and concerned, not only for their current state but also for their future. 'Course their future might not be all that long if the murdering scoundrels who'd attacked the Harris wagon were still nearby. He got to his feet and studied his surroundings. Seeing nothing, hearing nothing to indicate a nearby camp, he tried to relax. Had Warren and Luke made it safely back to the wagons?

"I don't feel right about taking your blanket." She shifted it from her shoulders. "We can at least take turns."

In the faint light from the moon, he looked at the blanket she held out. "I'm not cold."

She laughed softly. "Then neither am I."

They couldn't see each other very well, but he didn't have to see her to know she was being foolishly stubborn.

"You have to keep Anna warm."

"I found a sweater in the bundle you brought and I've wrapped my skirts about her."

The silent battle continued. "Look, Judith, I am not going to take the blanket while you and Anna sit exposed to the cold."

"Fine. But then I insist you sit close enough we can share body heat."

Again, he felt her insistence. Like that of the camp dog gnawing on a bone. He allowed himself to acknowledge how cold he had grown. "Person shouldn't be traveling this late in the season."

"And yet here we are." She patted the ground beside her. "Seems if a person is foolish enough to be on the trail this time of year it would be wise to take advantage of every offer of warmth."

"I guess I could help keep the baby warm." He sat beside Judith, their shoulders pressed together.

"Warmer?" she asked.

"Yes, thanks." A breeze pushed at his hat. He angled his body to provide more protection to Judith and Anna. In a few minutes, her head tipped sideways and her breathing deepened. She slept, the weight of her against his side.

He wouldn't sleep because of the need to stay alert for any hint of intruders.

"TRAPPER, ON YOUR FEET."

Gil awoke to the harsh sound of his name. Something weighed him down, preventing him from bolting to his feet as was his normal response to a sudden awakening. Judith lay across his chest. Anna curled into the crook of his arm.

He groaned. This did not look good.

Judith wakened and sat up, leaving him cold and exposed.

Anna opened her eyes, stared at the crowd of strangers and puckered up her face to cry.

Gil handed Anna to Judith and got slowly to his feet, vainly using the time to come up with an explanation that would satisfy those watching him. Warren and Luke wore matching hard expressions. Buck looked less shocked. He accepted that people sometimes had to make difficult choices. Did they have to bring along Reverend Shepton and Warren's friend, Sam Braddock? Too many witnesses. Too many opinions about the situation.

"I expect you to do right by my sister." Warren took his role as eldest brother far too seriously.

Luke nodded. "Her honor has been compromised."

"It was all innocent." They'd simply crowded together for warmth and then fallen asleep. It wasn't the least bit like Lillian in the arms of another man, her hair tousled, the buttons on her shirtwaist askew. In that case, the brothers might have cause for concern about Judith's reputation.

Warren held up his hand. "I know what I saw."

"You saw us trying to keep warm and keep this baby warm."

Everyone spoke at once, demanding to know

where they'd found the child, why they hadn't come back to the wagons, and insisting Gil must marry Judith.

He waved them to silence and choosing what he considered the most important of the questions, he explained about the Harris situation.

"It all seems reasonable to me," Buck said.

Gil shot him a look of gratitude but Warren and Luke took a step closer, their angry expressions in sharp contrast to Buck's calmness.

JUDITH HAD her hands full trying to soothe Anna. She found half a biscuit in the sack from which they had eaten last night and offered it to the child. Anna sucked on it. Poor little thing hadn't had a decent meal in twenty four hours or more from all indications.

She shifted Anna to one hip, liking the familiar feel of it. She'd done the same for her baby sister and for Warren's little son. But now was not the time to be reminiscing. Besides, it wouldn't be long before Luke and Judith's daughter, little Elena, would be big enough to cart around like that.

With three firm steps she placed herself between Gil and her brothers. "I have no desire to get married and you can't make me."

Her brothers' scowls deepened.

Buck did his best to hide a grin while Reverend

Shepton cleared his throat as if he had an opinion on the matter.

Judith didn't care to hear his opinion. Or anyone else's for that matter. She had to make herself clear. "After Frank died I decided I would never marry." She wouldn't even attempt to explain how devastated and disillusioned his death had left her. How empty she felt. Marrying another man would never fill that emptiness.

Warren made a dismissive noise that seemed particularly aggravating which might be, in part, due to the fact given that she was out of sorts. Disheveled and in an awkward position. And what she wouldn't give for a hot, strong cup of coffee. "I'm hungry," she said, hoping to make them all realize there were more important things at stake.

Luke smiled as if trying to convince her to be reasonable. "No one is saying you have to love him. But your situation means you have to marry."

She would have jammed her fists to her hips but her arms were holding a baby. She jiggled Anna higher. "No one needs to know we spent the night together unless one of you plans to say something." The look she gave each man was meant to warn them she expected compliance.

Reverend Shepton shook his head, his countenance full of sad regret. "Unfortunately every man and woman on the wagon train knows the two of you were missing and whether or not we say anything, they will come to their own conclusions when we return."

"He's right," Warren said in his most commanding voice. "There is only one remedy."

"He's right," Luke added in a more conciliatory tone. "Gil's a nice guy. He'll treat you right."

Her brothers turned to poor Gil and fixed him with twin scowls, silently warning him he better treat their sister right or answer to them.

Judith had an urge to stamp her feet but knew it would make her look petulant. "I have no wish to be married." Why was no one listening to her?

Anna had finished her biscuit and grown tired of the drama of the adults. She leaned her head against Judith's shoulder and wailed. At least the sound stopped all the silly talk about marriage. Judith meant to use the situation to her advantage.

"She's hungry. Can we go to the wagons and forget all this nonsense?"

They stopped talking and looked guilty then scrambled for horses. They'd brought an extra one for her. Gil seemed to be the only one who realized she needed a hand up. He took Anna as she mounted.

"I'm sorry about all this."

She reached for Anna. There was no way she was going to marry the man. Or any man. Nor would she let her brothers force her to. She had something more important to do—find Frank's brother—his step-brother—and inform him of how his dishonesty had destroyed Frank.

But she also meant to keep Anna. The baby fit right into her arms, right into the depths of her heart.

Could she pursue her quest and still persuade Gil to let her keep the baby? At the same time, put off her brother's demands. It was a heavy load.

As they rode toward the wagons, she considered how to accomplish her tasks.

She ignored the continued admonitions of her brothers as they covered the miles. Gil also held his peace even though the men informed him of their expectations.

By the time they returned, she had a plan.

Gil rushed over to help her down.

Once she was on her feet and the baby perched on her hip, she glanced about, saw that the others were occupied with unsaddling. Now was the time.

She caught Gil's arm before he could lead her horse away. "I will marry you," she murmured, not wanting anyone to overhear her. "On one condition."

His eyebrows twitched but other than that he gave no indication of how he felt about her announcement. "I suppose you're going to inform me of the condition."

"You let me keep Anna."

He considered her without any change in his expression which annoyed her no end. How could she tell what he was thinking?

"I promised Mr. Harris to see his little girl got a family."

Was he really going to deny her this after she'd

swallowed a large lump of pride in order to ask? "Wouldn't we be a family?" She could barely get the words out. Her idea of family would be like the one she'd grown up in—a mother and father who loved and supported each other, siblings who looked out for one another. However, the opportunity for that had passed with Frank's death. The way he died had left her unable to think of trusting her heart to another man. Frank had taught her to keep her heart locked up, safe in her own hands.

"I haven't had a chance to ask Luke and Donna Grace if they would take her and raise her."

Behind him, Luke and Donna Grace's baby, Elena, cried. Donna Grace looked weary. "Elena is only two weeks old. Neither of her parents are getting much sleep. Do you really think it's fair to burden them with another baby?"

She saw the uncertainty in Gil's face and pressed her point. "I'm guessing little Anna will need lots of extra attention. Surely she will be fussy from missing her parents."

Gil still looked unconvinced.

Fine. She wouldn't beg further. She was prepared to marry a man simply so she could keep Anna but her pride—or was it self-preservation—drew the line at lowering herself to the point she became a person of little value. Frank had taught her the pain of that.

"Forget it. I can see how unappealing you find the idea."

"I've been thinking. You're right about Luke and

Donna Grace and there isn't a lot of selection on the wagon train or along the trail."

The man spoke slowly and thoughtfully. In other circumstances she might have found that admirable, but at the moment, it simply caused her to feel as if she had vanished into the air.

He nodded. "I suppose you and I marrying would constitute a family for Anna."

She thought it was what she wanted. Thought she was willing to marry to give Anna a home. Now the idea seemed foolish.

He adjusted his hat and looked past her into the distance. "She deserves more than a pretend family."

"It sounds like you don't think it's a good idea." She took a step away ready to abandon the idea. But then what happened to Anna? Would Gil decide to hand her off to the first 'real' family that came along? The thought sent sharp talons into her muscles. She wanted Anna. She cared about the child. More than that, she knew Anna would not understand being shifted about. One loss was bad enough. More was beyond horrible.

She stopped and gave Gil a hard look, silently challenging him. "Anna should not be shuffled around."

"I agree, but you made it clear you don't want a man in your life."

"I lost my fiancé. The circumstances of his death make me understand I would never put myself in such a vulnerable position again."

His eyes narrowed as if her words had struck a

chord in him and made her realize how little she knew about him. "You also said you weren't interest in marriage."

"If we marry I would want to be a real father."

She tried to digest this information. "Exactly what do you mean?"

He shrugged. "I, too, have my reasons for not wanting a woman in my life. I once planned to marry, but the woman turned out to be unfaithful." He drew closer. "If you are serious about this, I have some conditions too." He paused, but she said nothing, waiting for him to lay out his part of the bargain. "I would expect your loyalty and respect. I would not tolerate regrets in any form but especially unfaithfulness."

They studied each other, taking measure, assessing what their proposed agreement would demand of them.

"I agree," she said after a moment's contemplation.

"Me, too."

Luke's wife, Donna Grace and her sister, Mary Mae, stood nearby, anxious and uncertain. Warren and Luke waited with arms crossed.

"They will marry," Warren said. "I will not allow my sister's reputation to be ruined."

Judith almost changed her mind. Warren had no right to make her decisions.

Gil took Judith's arm and guided her forward. "We have agreed to get married."

Judith chuckled at her brothers' surprise. It did her heart good to see them flounder for a response.

The reverend's wife hustled forward. "A wedding. How lovely." She looked at Anna. "And this is the little one you found. What a sweet baby."

Judith told them Anna's name while the baby sucked her two fingers and studied the circle of people.

Mrs. Shepton pressed her hands together. "You need to get ready for your wedding."

Judith glanced down at her skirts, realizing how rumpled she was. Her hair must be a mess too. And little Anna could do with a wash and change of clothes. Her stomach rumbled.

"Could we have breakfast first? I'm starved to a shadow."

"Of course. What are we thinking?" Mrs. Shepton turned her attention to the coals of the morning fire.

Little Polly, ten year old daughter of Warren's friend, Sam, trotted over. "Hi, baby."

"Her name is Anna."

"Can I hold her?"

"Yes, you may. She can walk." But Anna clung to Judith. "Maybe after she's eaten." Judith sank to the ground, Anna on her lap, and took the cup of coffee Mrs. Shepton offered. Ah. Just what she needed to steady nerves that danced like water on a hot stove. She sipped a mouthful then set the cup aside to tend Anna.

Mary Mae filled a bowl of oatmeal and handed it to Judith along with a spoon.

Anna drooled at the sight of food.

"Poor hungry little girl," Judith crooned as she offered a spoonful of the mush to Anna. She laughed at the way Anna's mouth popped open and how she leaned forward after each swallow.

Gil sat across from the fire pit, consuming his breakfast. He seemed mesmerized by the flames of the fire.

Judith spared him a glance or two as she fed Anna. She'd been comfortable with him since they met when the wagon train departed Independence. He seemed steady, reliable and kind. But she'd never seen him in the role of her husband. Now she was less certain about his character. Was there some reason the woman had been unfaithful? Guilt washed through her at how easy it was to assess and judge. She knew better. Hadn't she done the same thing to herself after Frank took his own life? And hadn't others asked the same questions? Made the same assumptions? She would not judge the man.

Anna stopped eating and toddled toward Polly, allowing Judith to dig into her own breakfast. Her coffee had cooled and she drank it quickly then wished she had lingered over it as her brothers hovered nearby, their purpose unchanged. They wanted to get the wedding over with.

Buck had ridden along the line of heavy freight wagons, all ready to depart, probably to warn them there would be a short delay. He returned. "Folks, I'd like to get on the way before the day is gone."

"We'll be ready shortly," Warren said. "Come on, Gil." The men led Gil away to get him cleaned up, they said. He glanced over his shoulder, a look of helplessness on his face.

She grinned and waved as the women urged her to her feet. Somehow, and she was reluctant to admit it to herself, it did her heart good to see him looking a little less than in total control.

Mary Mae, who had spent many nights in the Russell wagon, found Judith's best dress and helped her put it on then brushed Judith's hair and fashioned into a roll about her head. Donna Grace put baby Elena to sleep in her wagon then returned with her mother's mantilla veil. Donna Grace had donned it for her marriage to Luke.

"I can't wear that." It hit Judith that it represented a union built on mutual love. Not that she'd be the first woman to marry for other valid reasons. And what better reason than to give Anna a family?

And eventually a home? The truth smacked her hard. Gil had been guiding on the Santa Fe Trail for a number of years. He wouldn't be wanting to settle down. She drew in a solid breath. That suited her fine. She would be mother to Anna, and happy enough to have a husband who paid a yearly or twice-yearly visit. Where would she and Anna live? She could go back to Independence. There were no memories of Frank in that place.

Or she could go on to Santa Fe.

Luke and Donna Grace had plans to go on to California and start a ranch. Maybe she'd go with them. She and her brothers had grown up on a farm in Missouri. Her time there had been full of rich, vibrant memories. Her dreams for the future had been of a home and family as full of love and joy as she'd known as a child.

Somehow, she vowed, she would give that to Anna.

Of course, Gil might have some opinion about where Judith would go. Something she would deal with when the time came. For now, she meant to marry and raise Anna.

"I want you to," Donna Grace said, holding out the mantilla.

Murmuring her thanks, Judith allowed Donna Grace to cover her hair with the lace.

Gil returned in the company of her brothers and Sam and Buck. He looked different without his customary cowboy hat and with his hair slicked back. His freshly shaven face gave him a leaner, younger look. How old was he? There were so many things she didn't know about him.

"You look nice all cleaned up," he murmured at her side.

"You too." She grinned at him to let him know she took no offense at his comment.

"Thanks. Good to know." He grinned back.

And then the reality of what they were about to do, robbed her of amusement. She chewed her bottom lip.

Now was the time to back out if she had any doubts. Warren and Luke stood on either side of her and Gil as if to prevent either of them from changing their mind and trying to escape.

She straightened her shoulders and lifted her chin. They might think they were forcing her to do this but she did it of her own free will.

She faced Reverend Shepton. This was going to work out just fine. After all, she'd seen lots of Gil in the weeks since they left Independence and knew him to be kind. Perhaps a bit on the quiet side. Not at all like Frank who had been full of life and laughter.

She pushed aside the stinging memory.

The thing Gil required of her—her loyalty and faithfulness—she could freely give.

Reverend Shepton called for the attention of their little group. In the background, the drivers watched, waiting, she supposed, for this to be over so they could get moving.

She and Gil said their vows before the reverend and then she heard the words, "I now pronounce you man and wife. You may kiss your--"

Gil grabbed his hat. "Time to get moving." He vaulted into his saddle.

Judith couldn't move. It had happened so fast. And ended so abruptly. Not that she wanted or expected a kiss. But he didn't have to act like kissing her would have been worse than kissing his horse.

She released the air from her lungs. Truth was she didn't know what she wanted or expected. She and Gil would both have to find their way together. Seeing as he was the scout and often absent, she foresaw life going on much the same as it had since they left on this journey except with the addition of a sweet baby girl in her life.

Buck swung to the back of his horse and rode toward the freight wagons calling, "Wagons ho."

Luke and Warren sprang to their wagons. Polly handed Anna to Judith and climbed up beside her father. Donna Grace settled beside Luke, baby Elena still asleep in the back. Mary Mae stood beside the wagon, ready to walk.

Judith shifted Anna to one hip and looked about. Her place had been in the Russell wagon. She drove it part time when Warren was busy with his freight wagons.

She was now Mrs. Trapper and she had no idea where she belonged. Gil had freight wagons though she couldn't say how many, but she wasn't about to ride one of them.

What nonsense. She was still a Russell and she pulled herself up beside Warren and settled Anna on her lap. If the child got restless, she could play in the back or Judith would walk and allow Anna a chance to stretch her wee legs.

Judith and Warren rode without speaking as Judith played with Anna, enjoying the baby babble. So far she'd heard only one word she understood—mama. Judith would enjoy helping Anna learn more words, just as she'd teach her to enjoy life while avoiding danger. She fingered the white blonde hair that was little more than a fuzzy halo at the moment. Soon it would be long enough to braid. Soon too, she would outgrow the few dresses Gil had found. When they reached Bent's Fort she would purchase fabric and make new ones. Anna would be beautiful in blue.

"Gil is a good man," Warren's words startled her from dreams and plans for a future shared with a little girl. She digested the comment for a moment.

"So was Frank." She'd first seen him standing outside the Bird store looking at a sign that read 'Opening Soon.' He'd looked so pleased with himself that she had stopped and despite the impropriety of speaking to a stranger, she'd asked,

"Are you about to open a new business?"

"Yes, ma'am. Frank Jones at your service." He'd given a courtly bow. He wore a dark gray suit with a patterned vest and tie. The hat he swept from his head was a pristine bowler. He was quite unlike the men she usually saw.

"What are you selling?"

"Right now everything in the store is free." He opened the door to reveal an empty interior.

She'd given a little laugh. "There's nothing but air in here."

"And it's all free."

"It's free outside your store too."

"True enough. All the good things in life are free."

He'd been such a happy-go-lucky man. He laughed at life and because of his attitude, she did too.

Which made his death all the more tragic. And the means so completely unexpected.

But she wasn't going to think about that part.

"Did you hear me?" Warren asked, pulling her attention back to the here and now. "I said, I wish I had known Frank better. I only met him when I was home in the spring."

"He was a good man." She didn't know why she felt she had to make Warren understand that. Except perhaps because Pa had spoken of his doubts when Frank's business never opened. Frank always had an excuse. The shipment had been delayed. Or something else had gone wrong.

"And yet he continues to spend freely," Pa had noted and it pained Judith that she could give no explanation to satisfy her father because Frank laughed off her questions about his finances.

"I'm sorry he is gone." Warren squeezed her hands. "I know how painful it is."

"I know you do." Warren had lost his wife and child so he understood.

Gil rode toward the wagon.

Anna saw him and gurgled excitement.

"She recognizes him," Judith murmured.

"Probably associates him with rescue." Warren called a greeting to Gil.

Gil fell in beside the wagon. "I'm going to ride ahead and catch up to the other wagon train. The Harrises might have been part of that train. They might wonder what happened to the family."

Judith pulled Anna closer wishing she could protect her from the awfulness of what had happened to her parents. No doubt she wondered at their absence. Judith fully expected the child would mourn in her own way and not understand why she was sad. When Anna grew older, Judith would find a way to tell her about her parents. That gave her an idea.

"Gil, find out as much as you can about them so when Anna gets older, we can tell her about them."

"I'll do that. I won't be back for the noon meal." He tipped his hat and rode away.

Judith stared after him. This was the man she'd married and she knew practically nothing about him. When would she get a chance to remedy that? Or did she even want to? Was it possible they could continue on as if the wedding vows of a few hours ago had never been spoken? He'd seemed as reluctant to marry as she. Her neck muscles tightened. What did he think their marriage meant? An ever more fearsome thought filled her brain. What if he found a family at the other wagon train? Would he change his mind about being married to Judith? About letting her keep Anna?

3

G il rode slowly back toward the others. The wagons were already circled for the night. If only he had better news.

Buck cantered toward him.

Gil reined in and signaled the other man to stop while they were still a distance apart. "We'll talk here."

"What's wrong?" the wagon master asked.

Gil relayed the news.

They both sat in silence for the space of a minute. Then Buck nodded. "We best tell everyone."

Gil stayed behind Buck as they rode toward to the circled wagons. As Buck spoke to the others, Gil dismounted and waited. Horrified faces turned toward him as they understood why Gil stayed forty feet away.

Judith, with Anna in her arms, stepped past the wagons and walked toward Gil. He guessed she tried to appear calm but the skin on her face looked like it had shrunk.

"Diphtheria?" The word ground from her lips.

"I'm afraid so. The whole wagon is ill. Or at least exposed."

"Is that what her parents had?"

"I don't know. It was a bullet that killed them. But we must take every precaution to prevent spreading it to the others."

She hugged Anna to her. "She's been exposed. If she gets it—" Her voice choked off.

Gil cupped his hand to the back of Anna's head. "We'll know in a few days. In the meantime…"

"I know. We have to stay away from the others until the danger is past or—" Her voice thinned to nothing.

"We're in this together. I will take care of both of you." He draped an arm about her shoulders and pulled her close, feeling suddenly protective in an unfamiliar way. Their marriage was fresh and still unreal in his mind. He'd agreed only because he felt obligated. Perhaps in the back of his mind he hoped to find a suitable family on the wagon train and persuade Judith to turn Anna over to them. Then they could dissolve the marriage as if it never happened.

That was no longer an option, but Judith and Anna were now his responsibility and he meant to do his best by them.

She shivered. "I will nurse you if you get sick." He

could hear her swallow. "You were so exposed when you took care of the Harrises."

It was true. He had carried the bodies to the graves he'd dug. He'd gone through their belongings. If they had the diphtheria, he had been thoroughly exposed. So had Anna. He'd heard the moans of the sick and the weeping of survivors at the distant wagon train. He stifled a shudder. For the sake of Judith and Anna, he must be strong.

His wife and child. Although he knew what the words meant, they held no meaning for him. Things had changed far too quickly for him to be able to feel any connection to them.

As the women transferred the belongings of the Russell wagon into the Clark wagon, Warren went out and got the mules.

"They will only leave enough for us to survive on," he told Judith.

"I understand. If we have diphtheria everything will have to be burned." She leaned into him as if needing something to hold her up. He stiffened his legs and steadied her.

Warren drove the wagon a hundred yards from the others then jumped down. He gave his sister a sad look, but stayed his distance. Gil and Judith waited until he had trotted away to go to the wagon.

While Gil unhitched the animals and tethered them where they could graze, Judith looked into the wagon. "Some bedding and clothing. They've sent food." She straightened, her hands full. "I'll make supper."

Someone—likely Warren or Luke—had sent a supply of wood and Gil soon had a fire going. Judith had put Anna down in order to prepare the meal and she toddled to Gil and chattered up a storm.

"Honey, I don't understand you." He turned to Judith. "Do you know what she's saying?"

"Sorry no. I just agree with everything and she seems happy."

Gil wondered if he looked as shocked as he felt at her words. "What if you're agreeing to something you shouldn't?"

Judith laughed, her eyes flashing and her mouth widening.

At least she could still find humor despite the situation and he admired her for that.

"How would I know?"

Anna patted Gil's cheek and he shifted his attention back to her. "She's the picture of health, isn't she, with her chubby cheeks."

"She still has her baby fat." Judith's hands grew still as she studied Anna. "I hate that her parents have died. I hate that babies die. It doesn't seem fair." She returned to stirring a cornmeal mixture that she poured into a Dutch oven and set over the coals.

Anna had crawled to his lap and started bouncing. He held her hands to keep her from falling. When she bounced up, she rumbled her lips and giggled.

Judith watched them. "There's nothing sweeter than a baby's laugh."

"I've seen babies before but I didn't know they could play games."

"No babies in your life?"

"None. I was an only child until my widowed father remarried and I gained an older brother. But no babies." Ollie was a year older and had never welcomed a brother. Not that he was unkind. Simply indifferent both to Gil and to their father.

"Did you learn anything about her parents?"

He settled Anna on his knees and gave her a spoon to play with so he could concentrate on talking to Judith. "The man that came out to talk to me said they were a kind and loving couple. Always ready to help others. He said Mr. Harris had shared his supplies with another couple who had lost theirs in a river crossing even though it left them short. According to this man they hoped to make it to California."

"Looking for gold?"

"I asked the same question, but apparently they hoped to find a bit of land and start a farm. He said the missus talked about taking in boarders to help with expenses."

"They sound like a nice couple." She checked the cornbread and decided it was done. She cut a piece and blew on it to cool it.

Before she did more, Gil reached a hand toward her. "Shall I ask the blessing?" He couldn't think why he hadn't prayed without thinking he should hold her hand but if he pulled back now she might misunderstand and think he didn't want to touch her.

She took his hand and they each held one of Anna's hands.

He let out a relieved breath as he bowed his heart, his heart full, but his mouth unable to voice any of his feelings. He cleared his throat. "Lord God of all the earth. I thank You for sparing this little girl's life." He had to pause to take a deep breath. "I humbly ask You to continue to do so. Thank You for food and shelter and warmth." He wanted to say something more, but the thought hovered at the fringe of his brain and then he blurted out, "Thank you we can give Anna a family. Amen."

He dropped Judith's hand. Or did she drop his? She seemed to move with sudden haste, pouring a gravy mixture over the cornbread and drawing Anna close to offer her a spoonful.

"You can help yourself." She nodded toward the food then brought her serious gaze to his. "Or do you expect to be served first? I'm sorry. I have no idea what you wish from me."

"Relax." He leaned against the wagon wheel. "I'll wait and we'll eat together when Anna is done." He considered her question another moment. "Why would you think I expected you to serve me? I'm perfectly capable of taking care of myself. Have been doing so for a long time. In fact, I thought you would have seen that I can take care of myself in the days you've been traveling with us."

Her gaze darted away. "Some men expect certain things of a wife."

He gave a shout of laughter that drew both Anna and Judith's attention. "I thought I made myself clear. I have no need of a wife. Our marriage has one purpose and that is to provide a family for little Anna here."

Anna turned back to the food and opened her mouth, waiting for Judith to fill it.

Judith's eyes were dark and full of mysteries. They considered each other a moment before she returned to feeding Anna. Shortly thereafter, Anna refused any more. Judith set aside the bowl and picked up two plates and two forks, handing one of each to Gil. She removed a hunk of cornbread and offered it to him.

"Thanks." Before she could spoon out the stew meat, he grabbed the spoon and offered her some.

"Thanks," she said.

They both sat back, he against the wagon wheel, she closer to the fire. He half thought of bringing out his knife and slicing the air between them. He could build an invisible wall with the tension-filled bricks he'd cut. Was there some way he could ease the strain?

"What brings you out on the Santa Fe Trail?" He knew her parents were both living. Even with a dead fiancé, he wondered why she didn't stay with them.

JUDITH HAD BEEN LOST in a thousand troubled thoughts. Had she done the right thing in marrying

Gil? Should she have considered other options? But the most troubling of her thoughts was the fear of diphtheria. She ignored Gil's question to ask one of her own. "What do you know about diphtheria?" Without waiting for an answer, she continued. "My mother told about an outbreak when Warren was small and how she feared he would get it. She said she didn't leave the farm for six weeks while the disease raged." The skin on Judith's arms pebbled with a forbidding chill. "She said forty-five children and three adults died in that community before it ended." She shuddered. "She said the children suffocated from gray membrane in their throat."

"Judith, it isn't always that bad. People survive."

She slowly brought her gaze to him. "Not the children." She watched Anna playing contentedly with a piece of wood slated for the fire then eased her gaze back to Gil. She didn't know what she wanted or expected but he was the seasoned traveler. Surely he could offer some sort of reassurance.

He watched Anna. "From what I know, it starts with a fever and sore throat. Looks much like a cold. She certainly looks healthy enough."

Judith bolted to her feet. "We can do nothing but sit here and wait." She watched the flames of the fire where her traveling companions sat and visited. The mournful notes of a mouth organ danced across the prairie and took up residence in her heart. "What if she gets sick?"

He stood behind her. She felt the warmth of his

body and despite herself, drew comfort from his calm strength. "First, we will pray she doesn't get sick and then, if she does, we will do our best to nurse her back to health." He moved forward so he could look into her face. "Do you believe God takes care of each of us?"

"I used to. I want to, but now it's not so easy."

"Because you lost your fiancé?"

"You lost yours too." Wasn't that what he said? Or had he only said she had been unfaithful? "Does that make you wonder if God is watching over us?"

"I struggled for a while then came to accept that He gives us a free will. So we can choose to turn aside from the right way. That doesn't change who God is."

She considered the idea. "You're saying God won't stop bad things from happening when we choose a wrong way? Doesn't that mean there are no second chances? What hope is there for us?"

"God gives us as many chances as we need. We simply repent and He forgives."

"Why am I telling you my doubts? It will simply give you more reason to see me as inadequate."

He caught her hands. "When did I ever say you were inadequate? All I've said is I expect you to be faithful to our marriage vows."

She pulled her hands free. "If something happens to Anna, we will have no reason to be married to each other. Then what?"

She was grateful for the dim shadows so she

couldn't see his expression better but she saw enough
to know her question had angered him.

"All I asked of you and you agreed to was that you
be faithful and yet, here you are already looking for a
way out." He stalked to the edge of the light of the
campfire and stared across to the others.

A dozen arguments crowded her mind. She'd only
married him so she could keep Anna. He'd been clear
that he didn't want the marriage any more than she
did. Whatever his fiancée has done to him, whatever
her act of unfaithfulness, it had hurt the man deeply.
Her heart softened toward him as she recognized the
same sort of sorrow in him that she carried like a
shield.

She wished she had words of comfort to offer him,
but she had been unable to find them for herself, and
certainly had none for another.

Still she took a step toward him, but Anna let out a
wail and they both rushed to her.

"Mama," Anna sobbed.

Judith scooped her up. "I wondered how long it
would be before she realized her parents were missing." She bounced the baby up and down. "Mama's not
here, sweetie."

Anna leaned from Judith's arms, reaching for the
wagon.

"Maybe she thinks her mother is in the wagon," Gil
said.

Judith took Anna to the back of the wagon. Gil lit
a lantern and brought it along. He held it over

Judith's head so Anna could see the wagon was empty.

Really empty, Judith thought. "All our belongings must be crammed into the other wagons. Will they leave my things behind if diphtheria takes me?"

"See, no mama," Gil said.

Anna wailed louder and thrashed about in Judith's arms until she could hardly hold her.

With an arm on Judith's shoulder, Gil steered them away from the wagon. "Sufficient to the day is the evil thereof."

Judith wanted to be annoyed at his quiet acceptance of things, but instead found herself calmed.

"No one has the diphtheria yet and we are going to pray." He set the lantern on the ground, took Anna in one arm and one of Judith's hands in his hand. "Lord God, maker of heaven and earth and all that is therein, healer and protector, the one who loves us enough to meet all our needs, I ask for Your protection over us against illness and evil. In Your name we trust."

Anna continued to cry and tried to throw herself from Gil's hold. He had not raised his voice to pray. Yet each word had carried power and conviction straight into Judith's fearful heart.

"Amen," she whispered and withdrew her hand.

Gil walked around the campfire murmuring reassurances to the distraught little girl. "You're safe with us. We'll take good care of you and someday build you a castle in the sky out of fluffy white clouds. You'll wear a crown of golden flowers and dance among the roses. You will be the fairest girl in all the land. Judith and I will be your new family."

His words, full of imagination, made her see a perfect future for Anna. One that she and Gil would be a part of.

Anna's sobs grew less frequent and then ended except for a catch in her breathing.

"I think she's fallen asleep," Gil whispered. "Do you want to lay her down in the wagon?"

Judith climbed inside, took the baby from him and settled her on the blankets. Her heart kicked in alarm. "She's awfully warm," she told Gil.

"She's worked up a sweat from crying."

Judith's heart calmed. "Of course." She waited a moment to make sure Anna stayed asleep then slipped from the wagon and gathered up the few dishes from their meal.

"I'll check on the animals." Gil disappeared into the darkness.

Judith stared after him feeling alone and adrift. What was to stop someone from sneaking in and robbing them? Or worse? Killing them like they had Anna's parents.

"Everything is fine out there."

She hadn't heard Gil return and squealed.

"Did I frighten you?"

"A little."

"Sorry. Next time I'll give a whistle."

"Not necessary. I was just thinking there is no hiding from those people who murdered the Harrises.

We have a fire. And Anna has cried. We might as well send off fireworks to announce our presence."

"We are close to the others though. That will give anyone pause to attack us."

"I expect you mean to sound reassuring but I know how easy it would be to slip in under cover of darkness." She looked past the wagon into the night, feeling very exposed. "Maybe we should make some sort of rope enclosure about this high." She indicated her knees. "That would trip them. Maybe hang on some cutlery and pot lids to make a racket and scare them away. At least waken us though I don't think I'll sleep a wink."

"Don't think you can stay awake for a week. That's how long before we're sure we're out of danger."

She couldn't help smile at his drool tone. "Maybe we can take turns staying awake."

"No need. Buck has posted a guard."

She jammed her fists on her hips and glared at him. "Why didn't you say so in the first place instead of letting me ramble on."

His low-throated chuckle rumbled inside her chest. "It was too much fun listening to all the things you were going to do." He chuckled again.

She smiled. "I did go on, didn't I?"

"Maybe a tiny bit, though it's reassuring to know what lengths you would go to make sure we're all safe."

She stared into the distant darkness. If only Frank had realized she would have stood by him and helped

him even though his stepbrother had stolen the money
Frank needed to get his supplies. "Not everyone would
agree."

"Who doesn't agree?"

She should not have opened that door. She could
never tell him, or anyone, the shame she felt at Frank
choosing death over standing by her side.

"I know what it feels to have someone be unfaithful. I gave you my word on that matter and I will stick
to it." Again, she had hinted at a conversation she
didn't care to have.

"Someone was unfaithful to you? Your fiancé?"

Before she had to find a way to deflect his question,
Anna screamed and they both rushed to the back of
the wagon.

Gil jumped in before Judith could pull her skirts
out of the way and he scooped up the crying child.

"Mama," she wailed, arching her back.

"She's warm," Gil said.

Judith's heart gave a sluggish beat. "Bring her out."
Gil jumped down. Judith pressed her palm to Anna's
forehead. Indeed, she felt hot.

"We must sponge her."

Anna wailed at being undressed. She wailed louder
when Judith applied wet cloths to her tiny body. Gil
held her as Judith continued her ministrations.

Finally, with a gulping sigh, Anna relaxed in Gil's
arms.

"She's fallen asleep," he murmured.

Judith sank back on her heels. "Poor baby. Do you

think it's—" She couldn't bring herself to utter the word that meant agony and death.

"Is it possible she's just missing her mama and papa?" he asked. "That's a mighty big loss for someone her age."

"For anyone any age," she said.

"Granted. I didn't mean otherwise, but she's too young to understand, yet old enough to think they must be hiding somewhere."

She had to agree. Anna had looked in the wagon. Insisted on going around the wheels and tongue. She'd even pointed toward the other camp as if her mama and papa were visiting over there.

Judith touched the baby's forehead. "She doesn't appear to be warm now. But is that from sponging her, or—?" She wished she could consult a doctor or a medical book.

They sat by the fire that was now glowing coals. Neither of them seemed inclined to add more wood. After all, it was long past bedtime. The flames across the way had died out. Everyone had settled for the night.

Everyone but Judith and Gil. Gil must have read her mind. "You might as well get some sleep. I'll hold her a bit longer."

Judith looked longingly at the wagon. It would be so nice to stretch out and rest but she feared to take her eyes off Anna.

"I'll stay here and try and get a bit of sleep." She got a blanket and pillow from the back of the wagon and wrapped up. She lay on the cold ground, wishing she had a fur robe under her like the one Luke had provided for Donna Grace, but of course, they couldn't risk having to burn it so she'd have to make do.

Gil tossed a bit of wood on the coals and soon flames provided some warmth. He leaned back against the wagon wheel, a blanket swaddling Anna.

For now, things were peaceful. She had barely closed her eyes when Anna began to cry again, plaintive sounds, demanding sounds, sorrowful wails.

Judith threw off the blanket and sprang to her feet.

Please, God, not the diphtheria. Not when she'd married a man simply to provide a home for this child and then promised to be faithful to him.

Please God. Don't let it be for nothing.

4

Gil pressed his hand to Anna's forehead as he'd seen Judith do. "She doesn't seem overly warm."

Judith hovered over them. "I hope she's just upset at her loss. Not that I like to see her so sad, but I know the end for that will be better than if she was sick."

Gil pushed to his feet and rocked the baby.

Anna screamed and reached for Judith. She took the fretful child and jiggled her, singing a lullaby she had learned from her mother.

After a moment, Anna calmed, two fingers in her mouth. Gil looked at their wood supply. Almost gone. "We'll have to ration wood until we reach the Arkansas." He lit the lantern for light.

Anna watched him with accusing eyes.

"I'm sorry, little gal. I wish I could make you feel better."

Judith crooned soothingly. Anna's eyes drooped.

"I think she's asleep," Gil whispered.

"I'm not putting her down."

"Try and rest." He moved the pillow toward her. She eased down and let out a sigh. He covered her with the blanket then settled himself with his head on his saddle and his old blanket over him.

He barely relaxed when he was jerked up at Anna's wail and slipped the baby from Judith's arms.

Judith sat up. "I'll take her."

"Get some sleep."

"I'll trade places with you in a few minutes." She turned over, folded her hands under her cheek and sighed.

He wrapped a blanket about Anna and walked up and down the side of the wagon, humming and murmuring to her. She fought sleep, unhappy and unsettled, but buried her head against his chest as if defeated by her sorrow.

His heart cracked open and bled at his helplessness. "Little gal, I wish I could do something to ease your pain but I can't. I couldn't even find a way to deal with my own other than to ride away." He realized it no longer hurt to think of Lillian's unfaithfulness. "Guess being on the trail heals broken hearts. Maybe it will do the same for you." He watched Judith sleeping. She'd been hurt too. Her fiancé had died. Something she'd said...skimmed over without allowing him to ask about it...pulled at his thoughts. Not everyone would think she would stand by them. What did she mean by that?

So many things he didn't know about her. And she didn't know about him. He supposed they had the rest of their lives to learn things if they cared to.

He'd been so lost in his thoughts that when Anna threw herself backwards, he almost dropped her. "Whoa there, little gal."

Judith pushed the blanket to her feet and stood up. "I'll take her. You get some rest." She touched Anna's forehead. "Thankfully she doesn't seem to be fevered." She lifted the baby from Gil's arms. "Go lie down."

She offered the Anna a drink of water then broke off a bit of biscuit and gave it to her.

Anna sucked on it and seemed content.

Weary from too many nights of broken sleep and too many sorrowful events, he settled again with his head on his saddle.

Seems he had barely closed his eyes when Anna screeched and he bolted to his feet. "What's wrong?"

Judith bounced the baby and rocked back and forth on her feet. "I don't know. How do you know what's wrong with someone too young to tell you?"

"Guess?"

Anna quieted a bit to listen to them then threw herself backwards and wailed.

"Poor little gal." Gil took her from Judith. "You'd think she'd be so exhausted she would sleep despite herself."

Flames flared across the way. "Freighters are up.

It's morning." She yawned. A second fire flared closer to them as Warren lit a fire for the travelers. "I wonder if anyone got sleep last night."

Buck rode toward them. "Is the baby sick?" he called from a safe distance.

"Not that we can tell," Gil raised his voice to be heard, setting Anna into another bout of loud crying.

"Mrs. Shepton would like to speak to you."

"I'll go," Judith said, and in the thin morning light, went toward the woman who waited outside the circle of wagons. Judith stopped after a few steps keeping a goodly distance away.

Gil strained to hear what was said.

"It's good to think the baby isn't sick." Mrs. Shepton called.

Judith gave a mirthless little laugh. "I'm sorry we kept everyone awake."

"It's not your fault. I venture to say Anna hasn't been weaned so is missing her mother for more than just her absence. I've prepared a sugar rag. I'll leave it here. See if that helps." The woman put something on the ground and then withdrew.

Judith hurried to the spot and picked up the object. She brought it back to their lonely wagon.

It was a piece of heavy linen fashioned to something the thickness of Gil's thumb and about half as long. "What is it?"

Judith grinned. "It holds a lump of sugar. Anna can suck on it and be soothed." She stuck it in Anna's open mouth.

The baby spat it out and wailed.

"Come on, try it." Judith put it in again. Again, Anna spit it out.

"Just a minute." Judith sprinkled water on it to dampen the material. She waited a moment until she was satisfied then again put it in Anna's mouth.

Before the baby could spit it out, she tasted the sweet and her eyes widened. She closed her mouth around the rag and sucked. Within minutes she fell asleep in Gil's arms.

He looked down at her peaceful face and something as strong as the prairie wind and as sweet as the sugar rag rose inside him. His heart had opened to love for the first time since he'd discovered Lillian in another man's arms. This love was not at all the same. This love was full and free, protective and pleased. All he wanted was to be to this child, a father, a provider. All he wanted was a chance to love her freely.

He lifted his gaze to Judith. She must have read something in his gaze for her eyes softened and a tiny smile curved her lips. If he knew her better he would be tempted to say she liked what she saw.

"I'll put her down." She slipped her arms around Anna. For a moment they both held the baby. She lifted her gaze to his. Something about the realization of his feelings for Anna had caused a crack in his heart, one that let some tiny, unfamiliar feeling escape. Or did the feeling enter? He couldn't say. Couldn't even say what to call the feeling. Nor if he welcomed it or feared it.

Judith took the weight of the child and carried her to the blanket she had used off and on throughout the night and settled her there. She stood over Anna for a second, making sure she would remain asleep.

Gil went to Judith's side and they watched over the baby.

Judith reached for Gil's hand. "We are all she has."

He squeezed Judith's hand. "We will take care of her. Together." They had exchanged marriage vows that seemed but distant bells clanging. This vow united them far more than those had.

Oxen mooed and mules brayed. Men called out to the animals. It was time to prepare for the day's journey. Gil slipped away. He had a job to do.

He brought in the mules and hitched them to the wagon as Judith prepared breakfast.

"It's ready," she said, and held out a cup of steaming hot coffee.

"Thanks." He hunkered down beside the fire. "That will be the last of the wood until we reach the Arkansas."

She handed him a plate of potatoes, corn dodgers, and baked beans. "Does that mean we will have cold camps?"

"It means we will burn buffalo chips." He grinned inside.

"Whatever do you mean?"

"Dried buffalo droppings."

She stared at him then narrowed her eyes. "You are joshing me."

His grin spread across his lips. "'Fraid not."

She looked past the wagon. "Where do we get these chips?"

"Out there. You pick up the dried ones. The drier the better. And watch for spiders and scorpions."

She shuddered. "Can I change my mind and go back home?"

Laughter began in the pit of his stomach and rumbled up his throat. "It's a fair walk."

She grinned. "And if I don't gather them?"

He assumed she was teasing. "We eat cold food. And go without coffee." He gave his cup a mournful look then lifted his gaze to Judith. He knew she liked her coffee and wondered if it would be enough for her to overcome her reluctance to gather buffalo chips.

She looked at her own cup, then sighed. "I can't bear the thought of no coffee." She looked toward the other camp fire where her brothers and the others hunkered down, eating their morning meal. "Maybe we could leave our coffee pot out there and beg someone to walk out and fill it." She sounded so desperate that he had to laugh.

"It's not that bad. You pull up your apron to form a big pocket and fill it up. You can do it while you walk beside the wagon." The women all walked a good part of the day rather than endure the hard seat of a rough wagon.

Her eyes brightened. "But I have to take care of Anna. How can I go out there and gather those things?"

He couldn't say why, but her continued argument about something that had to be done and had been done by everyone else on the trail, amused him no end. "I'll keep Anna while you do that. Or she can run and play."

Judith snorted. "She can barely walk." Her eyes narrowed. "Besides, I would hate to lose her out there."

He chuckled. "Take a good look about you. The grass is so short you can see a snake fifty yards away."

She brought her gaze back to him and he almost choked at the way her eyes flashed with teasing. "If I see any snakes I will spend the rest of the trip in the wagon with a gun handy."

He'd been about to swallow some coffee and sputtered on it as he pictured her riding in the back watching for an intrusion by snakes. "What about the scorpions? You gonna shoot them?"

She looked about. "I'll whack them with a shovel." She shuddered and he knew it wasn't pretend.

"Be careful. Watch for them."

"How dangerous are they to children?" They both turned toward the sleeping baby.

"I heard it was bad for little ones."

They looked at each other, Judith's expression sobered, her eyes darkened. "First, she is orphaned, then we learn the diphtheria is killing those she traveled with and now I have to be on guard against snakes and scorpions. How do parents not worry themselves to death?" She shivered so hard that he eased to her side and patted her hand.

"We're in this together and we have a Heavenly Father to guide and protect."

She pressed her hand over his where it lay on her arm. "Thank you for the reminder. I may need to hear it constantly."

"I'm here to remind you." He'd enjoyed teasing her so much and seeing her reaction to the necessity of gathering the distasteful burning material that he'd failed to tell her they would soon reach the Arkansas River and wood for the fires. Now he thought it best not to admit his neglect. "Go easy on the water too. There won't be any more for a day or two."

Side by side, they finished eating breakfast then, while she cleaned up the cooking things, he stowed his saddle in the wagon.

There were ready to depart and stood over Anna as she slept peacefully. Two fingers had replaced the sugar rag.

"I hate to disturb her," Judith whispered.

"Wagons ho," came Buck's call and the rumble of heavy wagons and dozens of oxen shook the ground.

"Do you want to put her in the back or—?" This was so new and unfamiliar to him. Ask him where the next watering hole was, how to fix a broken wagon tree or even where to find mushrooms after a rain and he could answer with surety. But how to care for a baby…well, he simply didn't know.

"Why don't I sit on the bench and you hand her up to me? She might stay asleep, exhausted as she is."

He grinned. "I like how firm your conviction is on this matter."

She answered his grin with one of her own. "Sleep wasn't something she wanted much of last night." Her gaze followed the moving wagons. "I hope we didn't keep everyone awake."

It was Anna's crying that would have kept them awake, nothing either he or Judith had done but he liked the way she made it sound like they were all in this together. A unit. A family unit.

She climbed up to the seat before he could pull himself from his bemused state. He gently scooped up Anna and lifted her up to Judith. The baby snuffled. Judith stuck the sugar rag in before Anna wakened. With slurping sounds the baby sighed into Judith's arms.

They traveled abreast of the other wagons in contented silence. Or perhaps exhaustion. Judith's head fell forward and she jerked up convincing him it was the latter.

"Do you want to go in the back and have a rest while she's sleeping," he asked softly.

"Shouldn't I be gathering buffalo chips?" she whispered, her lips curling back as she spoke.

"There'll be plenty of time when we stop for the evening."

"Okay. That gives me a few hours reprieve." She glanced over her shoulder. "Then maybe I'll have a rest."

He'd have to stop to let her get down and go around back and he pulled back on the mules.

Anna struggled to sit up and looked about her sleepily. She looked at Gil and then Judith and her bottom lip trembled.

Judith offered the sugar rag and Anna sucked it eagerly but her accusing gaze went from Gil and back to Judith several times then she tried to escape Judith's arms.

Judith kept her from falling. "It's okay, little one. We'll take care of you."

Anna struggled to free herself.

"Forget having a rest," Judith said. "She needs my attention." Judith gave him a look half regretful, half mocking. "Not that she wants it at the moment."

Anna had slept through breakfast but Judith had prepared food for the baby and offered it to her now. Anna took a biscuit but didn't take a bite.

Judith pulled the rag from her mouth but Anna grabbed it and stuffed it back in. Her eyes flooded with tears.

Gil had to do something to ease Anna's sorrow. He could think of nothing except telling her about the trail and so he began to talk. "Anna, see the mules. They hear you and wonder who you are. See how that one flicks his ears. Hey, mule," he called. "This is Anna."

Anna's eyes widened and she looked at the animals with interest.

"That mule's name is Brighty because he's so smart.

And that one is Lefty because he is always on the left side." He continued talking about the mules, giving them far more personality than they deserved and telling of adventures they hadn't had.

It was worth it when Anna pulled the rag from her mouth and ate the biscuit and then the fried potatoes Judith offered her.

With the baby now content, he stopped talking.

Judith relaxed too. "Are you supposed to be scouting?"

He'd wondered how long it would be before that little detail began to bother her. "That's my job but for now, I'm here. One of the freighters is looking after finding camping spots."

"And keeping an eye out for murdering robbers, I hope."

"Yup."

He had so many questions for her. But did he have the right to ask them? He returned to one that he'd asked and she hadn't answered. "What brings you out on the Santa Fe Trail? It's not the usual place for an unmarried woman."

"I'M A MARRIED WOMAN," Judith said, enjoying the surprise and embarrassment that chased across Gil's face. "And you're the fortunate man I'm married to."

He slanted a look toward her. "Doesn't seem real, does it?"

She shook her head. "I keep expecting to wake up and find it's a dream."

He grinned. "So I'm the sort of man to fill a woman's dreams?"

She laughed softly. "Be grateful I didn't say I thought I was in a nightmare." Before he could take offense, she quickly added. "My nightmares are never full of handsome men offering their hand in marriage. More often they contain snakes and scorpions." She shuddered at the prospect of encountering either. She might be joshing about the subject, but they truly filled her with paralyzing fear. "In my nightmares I can never run or scream as the horrible creatures come after me."

"Handsome men? Nice to know I fall into that category." He looked supremely pleased with himself.

It took her a moment to realize what he meant. She'd used the term generically, not meaning him specifically, but she liked seeing the way the announcement softened his face. As if something inside him had opened up. She sat back as pleased as he.

"You're pretty good at deflecting my question."

"I am? What question is that?" She hoped he would ask something less demanding.

"What brings you on the Santa Fe Trail?"

"Oh that? Isn't it obvious? Two brothers, a covered wagon and half a dozen mules." She waved her hand dismissively.

He laughed outright, the sound causing the mules

to flick their ears and little Anna to stare at him. She pulled the sugar rag from her mouth and grinned.

For her part, Judith knew a sense of satisfaction both out of making him laugh and feeling the rumbling sound echo in her chest. She faced forward, uncertain if she wanted him to know how much she enjoyed the moment.

"Deflecting again," he said, humor and resignation coloring his words. "Are you going to make me try and guess?"

"If you like." She couldn't explain why the idea so amused her except that it would help pass the long hours of the day.

"Let's see. You said your fiancé had died. So I'm guessing you're running from that pain. I know it's what drove me to trading on the Santa Fe Trail."

Her mind buzzed with questions of her own. "Did your intended die as well?"

"She isn't dead as far as I know." The harshness in his voice made her want to stop her ears. But she couldn't keep from asking,

"Then what happened? I don't understand."

"I found her in the arms of another man."

"Like Warren and Luke found us?"

"Not at all. It was far from innocent."

Her cheeks burned at what he meant. "I'm sorry. So you left?"

"It was the main reason." Still that hard, bitter tone.

"What other reasons drove you from your home?"

"It's no longer important."

She touched his arm. "But it was at the time?"

"With my okay, Pa had taken my wages and put them back into our business. We had a dry goods store. The plan was to start another business closer to the trails. I would get my money back when the time came. But it was my brother who set out to start the new business. I expected my share of the money would still be available. But when I wanted to leave, I discovered I had no money. Pa had given it all to my brother and our business was mortgaged to the bank." He shrugged. "I felt betrayed at the time but I've gotten over it and made my peace with Pa." He grew silent a moment. "I'm glad I did because he passed on two years ago."

"I'm sorry about your loss. But it's good you were able to forgive him."

He jerked about to face her. "How did you know I had to forgive him?"

"It's pretty obvious to me. I'm working on forgiveness for both myself and for someone else."

"Are you hoping to find the person you want to forgive in Santa Fe?"

"You could say that." She would confront Frank's stepbrother, tell him what a rotten scoundrel he was to steal Frank's money and then she would be free of the pain of his sudden death.

For a time they rode on in silence except for Anna's baby babble.

To the right of them, the wagons pulled to a stop. The freighters dug into their larders and pulled out food. Warren, Luke and the others from the smaller wagons gathered together to eat.

Gil stopped the wagon and jumped down then hurried around to take Anna and put her on the ground. She toddled about, glad to be on her feet. He helped Judith down. She pulled out the cold meal while Gil took the mules to graze. The grass was dry providing limited feed. He filled a bucket from the barrel of water and gave the animals a drink.

She had the meager meal ready to eat when he returned.

Like the other men nearby, as soon as he'd eaten, he stretched out by the wagon, pulled his hat over his head and soon snored.

Judith would have liked to nap as well but she had to keep an eye on Anna who climbed over the wagon tongue and explored every little rock. It kept Judith busy keeping things out of her mouth.

All too soon it was time to move on.

Gil bounded to his feet, stretching and yawing. He adjusted the hat on his head and brought the mules back to the wagon. Finished with the animals, he turned to Judith. "Do you think little Anna will nap?"

"I would hope so. I'll climb in the back with her." Judith couldn't wait for the chance to stretch out her weary limbs.

She lay down and pulled Anna to her side. The little girl sat up and scowled at Judith.

"Mama," she demanded. It was clear to Judith that

Anna held her responsible for her mother's disappearance.

"I know," she crooned. "It's too bad. But if you have a sleep you will feel so much better." Judith yawned. She'd certainly feel better if *she* slept and she hummed a little lullaby. *Please go to sleep.*

Anna's eyelids drooped.

Judith hummed and waited.

Anna jerked her head up and widened her eyes, but she couldn't resist sleep and slowly folded down over Judith's chest. Judith waited, not wanting to waken her. Slowly, gently, hardly daring to breathe, she eased Anna to the quilt and released a quiet sigh when the baby stayed sleeping.

Judith immediately fell asleep and jerked awake some time later as the wagon jolted across a buffalo trail.

She glanced at the Anna who still slept peacefully, curled up into a little ball, the sugar rag forgotten in favor of her two fingers. Poor little baby. She missed her parents and could not understand why they were gone.

The nap had refreshed Judith, strengthened her to face her new life. She eased away from Anna and made her way to the front of the wagon where Gil sat. She rested her arms on the backrest. "How long did I sleep?"

His shoulders twitched as if her presence startled him.

She studied him. "Were you sleeping?"

"Not exactly."

She flicked her hand across his shoulder. "Not exactly? What does that mean? Aren't you either asleep or awake?"

"You can be both."

She guffawed. "How is that possible?"

"I can be half asleep."

"You mean one eye is asleep, the other awake?" This sort of conversation reminded her of the nonsensical conversations she'd had with Frank who had always found the humor in every situation. Her amusement fled. Frank had proved to be good at fun and laughter, not so good at trials and challenges.

"It's a skill that takes years to perfect," Gil said with a degree of superiority.

She chuckled. "Maybe I'll develop the same skill by the time we complete this trip."

He didn't reply and she settled her chin on the tops of her hands. Her thoughts began to circle. Gil was her husband. She still couldn't believe it to be real. What did she know about the man besides he and her brothers had traveled together many times and they spoke highly of him? She'd had a chance to learn little about him since they'd left Independence. He was often gone scouting, but had sometimes joined them for the evening meal. He was always quiet and thoughtful, ready to help where and when needed. Seems she should know a little more if they were to be man and wife. Father and mother to the wee girl in the back.

No better time than the present to learn a bit more. "Don't I remember you saying your father was a widower?"

"My own mother died when I was five. I don't remember her at all. When I was ten, Pa remarried and gave me a stepmother and a stepbrother. I was happy to finally have a family. Until then I had always accompanied Pa to the store. It was the only home I knew. My new ma gave me a home."

"Did you get along with your stepbrother?" Frank talked about how he'd always felt his stepbrother was favored by both the father and the mother.

"We weren't best friends, but we got along alright."

"Yet your pa gave him your share of the money. Doesn't that make you bitter?" Having his stepbrother steal Frank's money had led her fiancé to despair. Live-ending despair.

"Pa thought it fair seeing as Ollie was older."

Ollie. She'd half expected him to say Frank, but of course, Frank wasn't the only one to have a stepbrother, and obviously not the only one to have money woes related to them.

The afternoon heat grew. "Isn't it hot for this time of year?"

"One thing I've learned on the trail is you can't predict the weather."

Judith leaned forward for a better look at the sky and the surrounding landscape. Nothing but blue sky. Beside them, the other wagons rolling slowly across the prairie, dust billowing up from hooves and wheels.

Mary Mae walked beside the Clark wagon. She glanced toward Judith and waved. Judith waved back, missing her friend. She'd been so preoccupied yesterday with caring for Anna and the shock of being married that she hadn't even discussed it with Mary Mae. Now she wished she could fall in step with the other woman and pour out her confusion and uncertainty.

Someone called to Mary Mae and with another wave, she turned her attention away from Judith.

Judith sank back on her heels.

Gil had seen the little exchange. "I'm sorry, but I'm the only company you will have until the danger of diphtheria is over." He shot her a teasing grin. "What shall I do to amuse you?"

She pushed aside her loneliness and uncertainty to study Gil's face as he watched, waiting for her reply. His dark eyes flashed with playfulness and then it fled, replaced with a soberness that made her nerves twitch. It felt is if he searched her thoughts. Perhaps wondering, even as she did, what sort of marriage their agreement promised.

It wasn't a question she could answer. She wanted to keep her heart closed to caring for a man. Did that mean they would live separate lives even when in the same house? Or would they find a way to be more than roommates? Heat started in her throat and headed for her cheeks.

Not wanting him to see, perhaps interpret her flushed cheeks to mean more than embarrassment, she glanced over her shoulder. "Anna is sleeping for now. But I don't expect the peace to last long."

"Poor little girl must be exhausted."

"I know I was." She brought her attention back to Gil who faced forward allowing her the opportunity to observe him openly. She was beginning to get a picture of him. A motherless child until age ten. And then his inheritance or wages or whatever he wanted to call it, given away to a stepbrother. Yet, unlike Frank, Gil chose to keep going, to find work he enjoyed, and to be a kind man.

Anna snuffled and sat up. Before Judith could reach her side, Anna wailed. Judith lifted the baby to her lap, found the sugar rag and tried to get Anna to take it.

Anna jerked it from her mouth and threw it aside. She pushed from Judith's arms, pressing herself against the wall of the wagon, as far from Judith as she could possibly get, fixing Judith with an accusing, angry glare. And she screamed.

"What's wrong?" Gil asked.

"She's an unhappy little girl." Judith reached for Anna. "Come on, sweetie. I'll cuddle you."

Anna screamed louder, shredding Judith's eardrums.

Judith offered the sugar rag. Offered her a dry biscuit. Tried to play peek-a-boo to distract Anna.

Nothing worked.

Gil stopped the wagon and came round to the back. He reached in and lifted Anna from the wagon.

Anna kicked and screamed.

"Looks like a temper tantrum to me," he said, raising his voice to be heard above Anna.

The others watched from across the way.

"She wants her mama," Polly called, when Anna paused to take a breath.

"Mama." Anna dissolved into heart wrenching tears.

"Poor baby," Judith crooned. "I feel so helpless. How do we comfort her?"

"I don't know." Judith and Gil looked at each other, sharing their concern for the little girl who now had no one but them to provide her needs.

"We need to do more than give her food and shelter," Judith said.

"Like what?"

"Comfort and love." She didn't know why she'd tacked on the last word and hoped he understood she meant love for Anna. Nothing more. Certainly not the kind of love a man and woman shared.

She couldn't tear her gaze from Gil's and wondered what he thought of her saying the child needed comfort and love. Did he think he needed it too? Or that she did?

Why had her foolish thoughts even considered such a thing?

5

G il studied Judith. He'd heard her words. Anna
needed comfort and love. "How are we to give
it if she rejects it?"

Judith blinked twice as if she wasn't sure what he
referred to.

Why would she be surprised, perhaps even
confused, at his response? Had he misheard her? No,
he was certain of what she'd said.

She looked at the baby squalling in his arms. "The
first thing is we must be patient with her."

"Of course. What else would we be?"

"Some would think a child having what appears to
be a temper tantrum should be spanked." She didn't
meet his eyes.

He caught her chin and turned her face toward
him, waited until she lifted her eyes and met his. "A
temper tantrum by a spoiled child is one thing and

might require some form of discipline." He couldn't imagine spanking a child as little as Anna though he knew those who did. "But one by a child who has lost her parents is quite another. I think it calls for compassion."

She nodded. "I agree. But it can't be good for her to continue crying like this"

The other wagons rumbled onward. Her friends marched ahead, leaving Judith and Gil and the crying baby in the dust from the trail. Buck rode up, stopping a distance from them.

"Is there anything you need?"

Anna's mother and father, Gil thought. But those roles now belonged to Judith and him. "We'll settle her before we continue," he called. Their lighter wagon would have no trouble catching up to the slower, heavier wagons. He stared down at the distraught little girl who alternately screamed and sobbed. "I have no idea how to calm her."

"I'll try the sugar rag again." Judith climbed into the wagon and returned with the soggy thing. She stuck it in Anna's mouth and held it there. Anna tried to push it out then with eyes streaming tears, began to suck.

Judith wiped away the tears and dried the little face. "I'll take her." But when she reached for the Anna, the baby clung to Gil, pressing her face to his shoulder.

"That's okay. I'll hold her."

"Why don't I drive," Judith said. "While you and

Anna ride in the back. Maybe you'll both be able to sleep."

The idea was tempting. His eyes were gritty from lack of sleep. But he wasn't comfortable enough with the situation to rest while Judith drove. He knew she could. Had witnessed her doing so. But to snooze in the back...

Well, it required a degree of trust to make himself so vulnerable and he wasn't able to do that. "Time to get moving." They returned to the wagon seat. He held Anna as he drove the mules. She played with the ends of the reins.

Gil looked at Judith, saw his relief reflected in her eyes. After a bit, Anna's head drooped. Gil shifted her so she slept across his knees, her head in the crook of his arm. After a bit his arm began to ache but he would not complain. "At least she is calm while sleeping," he murmured.

Judith didn't seem inclined to make conversation so the afternoon hours passed in quiet watchfulness of the passing scenery that changed very little. They would soon come to the Little Arkansas River and fresh water and wood to burn. He smiled at the memory of Judith's reaction to burning buffalo chips. If they were going the way of the Cimarron cutoff, they would find neither wood nor water. Instead, they were going by way of Bent's Fort. He might sell the contents of his three wagons there, rather than go on to Santa Fe, and take the money back to his stepmother and his other obligations.

The wagons beside them stopped at a familiar camping spot. They circled into place.

He pulled their wagon to a halt. Judith looked around. "We're camping here? I don't see any water."

"No water. No wood until we reach the river."

She glanced to their left. "How far will I have to go for fuel?"

"Buffalo chips?" He couldn't keep the teasing out of his voice. "You'll need an apron full to make supper and breakfast." He jumped to the ground, the movement waking Anna.

She opened her eyes and looked about, gave a little sob but nothing more. Thinking she might want to stretch her legs, he put her down.

Judith joined him and they watched Anna toddle about. "I better be getting that fuel." Judith took Anna's hand and they headed out to the prairie.

Grinning at the determined look on Judith's face, Gil unhitched the mules, gave them water from a bucket and hobbled them where they could graze. He kept them as close to the wagon as possible for even though Buck had the guards check on Gil and Judith, Gil knew they were, as Judith said, easy prey. But the mules were good guards too. They would bray at anything unusual.

He returned to the wagon, but Judith had not come back. He tented his hand over his eyes and looked across the prairie until he spotted her some distance away, her apron bulging with her pickings. He squinted to focus on the distance as he looked for

Anna. She'd wandered away from Judith but Judith seemed not to notice. He stared some longer. Judith didn't move. She didn't pick up buffalo chips. Nor look toward Anna who got further and further away.

A shiver raced across Gil's neck as he sensed something amiss. He grabbed his rifle and trotted toward her. If thieves hid in a depression where he couldn't see them, he knew he couldn't hope to approach unnoticed, but there wasn't any way to avoid that. His only protection was to move fast and dart from side to side so he didn't make an easy target.

He stopped fifty feet from her and fell to one knee, the rifle aimed to any danger in front of her.

He held motionless and alert for several seconds. Nothing moved. Nothing signaled danger and he rushed to her side. Her face had lost all color.

"Judith, what's wrong?"

She didn't move. He couldn't say if his question even registered.

"Judith?"

The sound that came from her throat was half groan, half sputter and she pointed toward a buffalo chip that lay a yard away, its underside exposed.

He looked about for a snake or tarantula. Saw neither. A quick glance informed him Anna had heard his voice and he made her way back to him. "Judith." He shook her slightly.

She blinked. Her eyes slowly focused on him. She shuddered.

"You're okay."

She tilted to one side.

He grabbed her. She clung to him as shivers raced through her body. He rubbed her back and made soothing noises. The shivers lessened.

"What's wrong?" he asked, his arms still about her.

"Snake," she whispered.

He looked again. Nothing. If there had been a snake it had slithered away. "Wait here." He raced toward Anna and scooped her up just in case there was something harmful lurking about. Judith wavered, as unsteady as a tree about to topple. He hurried back to her side and wrapped an arm about her shoulders, holding her close and upright as they made their way toward the wagon.

Half way there, she straightened. "I hate snakes."

"I guessed that."

"Is this enough fuel?" She indicated her apron.

"It will do." There'd be enough for preparing the meals. But if they wanted a hot breakfast there be no evening fire to chase away the chill. But then he'd survived worse. Little Anna had too and he'd be sure to keep her warm.

They reached the wagon and Judith emptied her apron.

"I'll start the fire," Gil offered.

"That's good of you."

The gratitude in her voice made him grin. "I'm basically a good person," he said.

She laughed softly. "I know."

Their gazes locked across the smoke from the

reluctant fire. Something warm and faintly familiar escaped from the depths of his heart. It took a moment for him to place the feeling. Judith's words of acceptance echoed the words of his step mother when she had married his pa.

"I know it isn't easy to suddenly have a mother," she'd said. "But I also know we will do just fine. I love you and that is enough."

He and Judith didn't have love. Seems neither of them wanted it. But they had Anna and the promise of a life together. That was enough. He turned his attention back to the fire and she concentrated on preparing a meal.

The fire caste a dim glow as they ate.

Anna perched on Gil's knees eating only if he fed her from his plate. It pleased him that she allowed this.

As they finished, lightening forked across the sky and thunder rumbled in the distance.

"Are we in for a soaker?" Judith asked.

"It's a long ways away." Still a cold wind fanned the embers of the fire and made him shiver. He carried Anna as he retrieved blankets from the wagon. He draped one about Judith's shoulders, another about his own and wrapped Anna tightly in the third.

Across the way, voices murmured in low conversation and then the freighter began to play his harmonica. Sad, slow tunes. Someone must have objected because he switched to lively tunes and two of the freighters stomped out jigs in time to the music.

Anna's head fell against his arm. "She's dozed off," he whispered.

"Good," Judith whispered back. "Hopefully she'll sleep through the night and we'll all get some much needed rest. Let's put her to bed." The fires across the way had died down and the music stopped.

He carried Anna to the wagon and waited for Judith to climb into it then handed her the baby. She hummed as she settled Anna.

Gil edged away silently. He placed his bedroll under the wagon, his rifle close at hand and was asleep as soon as his head hit the ground.

JUDITH LAY with Anna's warm little body beside her.

Warm? She touched the baby's forehead. Was she too warm? In her stupid fright about the snake she'd forgotten about the threat of diphtheria. She wasn't much of a mother.

But she would get better. She'd be the best she could be.

The statement failed to bolster her faith in herself. She'd been the best she could be for Frank and it wasn't enough. Not enough for him to face the challenges in his life or even to realize that she would stand by him no matter what his future looked like.

She pushed aside the regrets. This trip would put an end to them. Just as soon as she found the stepbrother and made him own his share of responsibility in Frank's death. She'd asked around and listened as the men talked but so far had not heard anyone with the name Jones that could be Frank's brother. One Jones was a little Welsh man. He didn't fit the sort of man she sought. Too old. Frank's brother was only a year older than him. Frank had never given his name, simply called him his stepbrother. Not until after his death and her decision to find him did she wish she'd asked.

She checked Anna again and decided she didn't have a fever. Six more days before they would be deemed out of danger. From beneath the wagon came Gil's soft snores. Beside her, Anna slept peacefully. The distant storm had moved out of earshot. For now all was right with her world and Judith asked God to keep it that way before she fell asleep.

The next morning, Anna still slept as Judith slipped out to start breakfast. Poor little thing had worn herself out with crying and fussing. Sleep was the best thing for her.

Judith made coffee and fried salt pork and corn dodgers as Gil brought in the mules. She'd restricted the coffee to one small cupful each as their water supply was limited.

"Anna still sleeping?" Gil asked as he joined her for breakfast.

"It's the best thing for her."

Gil asked the blessing. "Lord God, thank You for yesterday's safe passage and that no one was harmed by the snake. Thank You for sufficient fuel, for food and water. Thank You that none of us is ill. Please protect us from such. Keep us all safe. Amen."

Judith admitted to herself she liked the way he prayed...as if he trusted God's care completely. She handed him food and helped herself. While they ate, she tried to find words to express her feelings without looking like an utter chump. "Gil, you've been through so much with your mother dying and lately your father, with the disappointment about your share of the money and the unfaithfulness of the girl you loved. And yet, you pray like your faith has not been shaken one degree by it."

He sipped his coffee and didn't speak for a moment.

She knew him well enough to know he considered his words before he spoke.

"Like you mentioned, I had to forgive those who hurt me. Once I learned how important that was, I found it easy to trust in God's unchangeable nature."

"How did you learn? Did something happen?"

He set his cup down and pulled one knee up to rest his hands there. "I made a very bad mistake when I was first on the trail. I was in partnership with an older fella by the name of Stu Macleod. He knew the trail but needed someone younger to help with the wagons so we worked together. We reached a river and I thought I could take the wagons down a short cut even though Stu was against it. He was far more cautious than I and knew it, so he let me make the decision to take that route. Turns out he was right and

I was wrong as I learned on my first attempt. The wagon upended and threw me forward. Stu saw what was happening and raced in on horseback to pull me out of harm's way." Gil stared into the flickering midst of the fire.

Judith saw the pain in his face and knew the outcome had been awful. "Did your friend die?" she whispered.

"No. He likely saved my life but his legs were crushed. He was in so much pain. We made a bed for him in the back of a wagon and splinted his legs as best we could. I did everything I could to care for him. And told him over and over how sorry I was." His voice deepened with regret.

"Stu was pretty much out of it for a few days. We gave him as much laudanum as we could but even so, he groaned at every rut we crossed."

Judith understood how Gil's mistake hurt him, but she wondered what it had to do with learning to trust God. She waited for Gil to continue.

Gil let out a gusty breath as if he'd forgotten to do so for several minutes. "Stu healed up but he would never again ride the trail. He took his share of the profits and bought himself a little house. He gave me the wagons. I said I couldn't take them. I didn't deserve them. I was responsible for his bum legs." Gil's eyes flared with a light that made Judith look at the fire to see if flames had shot up. They hadn't. Gil's fire came from within.

"Stu said to me he wasn't giving me the wagons

because I deserved them or didn't, but because he considered me his partner and because he didn't blame me for a mistake made without malice. I still wouldn't take them. Then he said he wanted me to think of them as a lesson about God's love. We don't earn it, nor can we quench it. The worst thing we can do is refuse it and that is the most foolish thing a man can do." Gil's smile was so sweet that it dribbled honey into Judith's heart. "That's when I decided to live a life free of bitterness and instead, trust God's love."

Judith brushed back a tear. "That's a beautiful story. Where is Stu now?"

"He has a home in Independence and seems happy. He has lots of company."

"Is he able to support himself?"

Gil ducked his head and twisted a bit of dry grass between his fingers. "He doesn't have to," he murmured.

"What do you mean?" And then she understood. "You take care of him, don't you?"

He lifted one shoulder. "I make payments on the wagons."

She reached over and squeezed his hands. "You are a good man." Likely one she could trust, but she wasn't ready to put her faith in that just yet.

"Wagons ho," Buck called and Judith and Gil both jolted to their feet and prepared for the day's journey.

"Anna is still asleep," Judith said. "I'll ride in the back until she wakens."

Gil held out his hand to help her into the back then went round to the front and prepared to drive.

Judith sat with her back against the seat, wanting to be close enough to talk to Gil but she couldn't find the words to convey all that was in her heart. He was a good man. She'd told him that. Perhaps if Frank's step-brother had been even a little like Gil, Frank might still be alive and she'd be back in Crestheight, Missouri, likely married to him. She wouldn't be on this journey. She wouldn't have become Anna's mother.

Nor would she be Gil's wife though she wasn't really that either.

She didn't want to think about what the word wife meant so began to talk. "Do you think Anna is okay?

"Do you think otherwise?"

"I don't know. Perhaps I'm a bit too eager to have her sleep. Should I be keeping her awake?"

He gave a dry chuckle. "Likely she's plumb wore out. Sleep is good."

Judith considered it. "I guess I can't help worry. I had a little sister, Dodi. Short for Dorothy but no one ever called her that. Even her tombstone said Dodi with Dorothy in brackets. She died about the same age as Anna is." She fell silent as memories flooded through her, good ones trampled by bad ones. "I loved her. She was six years younger than me. I played with her like a little doll." Her voice caught. "She imitated everything I said and did. When she was six months old I taught her to rumble her lips like this." She illustrated. "Oh, how I loved her." The words scraped from her throat, leaving it raw.

Gil reached back and squeezed her shoulder.

She needed his strength and grabbed his hand, holding on like he was a lifeline and she a drowning woman.

"One day we were in town. Mama and Papa had gone to speak to someone and left us in the wagon to wait. A friend of Luke and Warren's came up with a puppy and they jumped down to see it. Just then a runaway wagon came barreling toward us. It hit the side of our wagon and threw me to the street. The wagon upset. I remember Mama rushing to us, screaming for Dodi and me. She saw me lying in the street. I guess she thought I was okay because she went to Dodi. Papa had to untangle the horses and sort them out and get the wagon back on its wheels. I think Luke and Warren helped. Mama sat on the ground holding Dodi and rocking back and forth, not crying but moaning. I remember someone shouting for the doctor and he came running. I remember people hovering about, wringing their hands and shaking their heads. The doctor bent over Mama and Dodi then came to me. 'We'll have you fixed up in no time,' he said, in such a kind voice. But my fears didn't end. It was the way Mama looked that frightened me. 'Is something wrong with Dodi?' I asked the doctor. He said, 'She's gone back to heaven.' Again, that quiet, calm voice which did nothing to end my fears. 'Heaven? She's...?' I couldn't say it. I knew what dead meant. I'd seen baby pigs that didn't live, but Papa never said they had gone to heaven.

"Someone led Mama away, still holding Dodi. Papa wrapped his arms about her shoulders. Luke and Warren stood nearby looking lost. They finally remembered me and came. 'I want Mama.'

'She'll be back,' Luke said.

"Warren gathered up our scattered belongings and put them into the wagon that had been returned to its wheels.

"The doctor splinted my leg and got someone to help him get me into the wagon where he covered me with a blanket. 'I'll be out to see you at home.'

"Papa led Mama back to the wagon. I don't remember if she carried Dodi or left her at the church. I was feeling a little sorry for myself.

"At home, Papa carried me into the front room and settled me on the sofa. The doctor came and checked my leg. Then went to see Mama.

"Everything kind of blurred together after that. Mama cried a lot. I knew that Dodi had died but it didn't seem real. I wondered if they were mad at me for not watching her better and that's why they wouldn't let me see her.

"Then they all left and I stayed home with a neighbor lady who came and brought me cookies. I realized they had gone to bury Dodi. The neighbor lady said 'Your mama will never get over this. People don't get over these sort of things. Don't be surprised if she never sees you quite the same again.'

"I didn't understand. Was I to blame?" She squeezed Gil's hand. "I guess like you, I blamed myself."

"Was your mother different?" His voice was low, full of sympathy that eased the memory back into the past.

"I was so afraid after what that neighbor lady said. Maybe Mama would not want to see me anymore. Maybe she'd miss Dodi so much she'd forget about me. But when she came home she came right to me and sat with my head in her lap." Judith knew her tone had changed to one of joy. "Mama took good care of me all the while I had to lie still for my leg to heal. She sang to me, she played with me and read to me and helped me memorize Bible verses. Our goal was a hundred verses as I waited for my leg to heal and I was so proud to reach that number. Mama was proud of me too. To this day, I remember those verses. And Papa and my brothers built me a doll house. I felt so cared for. Strange that from that awful event I have some of the sweetest memories."

"Like Stu told me, God doesn't waste bad things. He uses them for our good."

Judith didn't remember moving, but she realized she knelt at the bench, her head on the same level as Gil's. He'd shifted so they looked deeply into each other's eyes. Why did she get the feeling he saw past the color of her eyes, just as she saw past the brown in his, to the deepest depths of her heart where there lived memories both good and bad. And somehow they had all turned sweet.

"Whoa." Gil pulled back on the reins of the mules.

"Why are we stopping?" She peered out the wagon and saw that the long line of wagons had also stopped.

"It's nooning time." He chuckled at her surprise.

Judith jerked around. "Anna is still asleep." She knelt at the baby's side and watched for her chest to rise and fall. When it did, she let out a relieved sigh. "She's still breathing."

Gil came round the back. "Maybe it's time to waken her."

Judith shook Anna. "Wake up, honey."

Anna did not open her eyes.

Judith rolled her to her back. "Anna, wake up."

No response.

"What's wrong with her?"

6

The fear in Judith's voice echoed Gil's own concerns and he jumped into the back of the wagon to bend over Anna. "Wake up, little one." He sat her up, but her head lolled to the side and she was as limp as a rag.

He carried her from the wagon with Judith on his heels.

Judith dampened a cloth and wiped Anna's face. The baby moaned at the cold, but didn't open her eyes.

Gil tried to make her stand. Anna opened her eyes and whined then folded to the ground.

Judith grabbed Anna and lay her on the ground. She patted Anna's chest, tapped her shoulder. Anna's only response was to put two fingers in her mouth and ignore all efforts.

Gil hunkered down at Judith's side. "How can she

sleep through all our prodding? How do we know if she's sleeping or—?" He couldn't bring himself to say unconscious. Besides, what would bring her to that state? He touched her forehead. "I don't think she has a fever."

Judith touched the tiny forehead too. "I agree." She sprang to her feet. "Someone over there must know." She dashed half way across the distance. "Mrs. Shepton, can I talk to you?"

The woman left the others and took half a dozen steps toward Judith then realizing she could go no further, stopped. "What is it?"

"Anna won't wake up. I don't know what to do."

Gil, at Anna's side, strained to hear Mrs. Shepton's response.

"What do you mean she won't wake up? Is she sick? Unconscious?"

"She doesn't seem to have a fever. She opened her eyes when we tried to make her stand then closed them again and lay down on the ground. She's sucking her fingers."

"Was she awake all night?"

"No, she's been asleep since supper."

"I have to say it mystifies me. It's hard for me to judge when I can't see her. I suggest you sit her up and see if she will drink a little water. I'll wait here to see how that goes."

Judith hurried to put water in a cup.

Gil held Anna upright in his lap and kept her head from tipping to the side.

Judith knelt in front of Anna but didn't offer the cup. "I'm afraid of choking her."

He eased Anna's fingers from her mouth. "Try tipping the water just to her lips."

Judith did so.

They both heaved sighs when Anna swallowed. Her eyes flicked open and then she turned her head away.

Judith returned to report to Mrs. Shepton.

Gil listened for the older woman's reply.

"I suggest you keep giving her water every few minutes and see if she doesn't come out of this on her own. I'm just guessing here, but I wonder if she's pulling into herself because she's missing her parents. We'll be praying for you." Mrs. Shepton rejoined the others who had listened to the conversation.

Luke and Warren stepped from the wagons. "Judith, are you okay?" Warren asked.

Gil felt Warren's warning glance, but ignored it. Judith's brothers had no reason to worry that he wouldn't take care of Judith. He took his vows and his responsibilities seriously.

Unfortunately, he'd learned not everyone did.

"I'm fine," Judith called. "Just worried about Anna." She waved to her brothers and rejoined Gil. She gave the little girl another drink.

"It's good she drinks, isn't it?" she asked Gil.

"It is." It meant she wasn't unconscious.

Judith looked about. "We have to eat and you need to rest while you can." She handed out the cold meal, her gaze lingering on Anna. "If only we had some milk for her."

"It will be Bent's Fort before we'll find that."

"What if she decides she is going to stay asleep?"

Gil ate two mouthfuls as he tried to ignore what she meant. "We'll find a way to make sure she doesn't."

"What if what we do isn't enough?" The bleakness of her tone, the agony in her face erased every vow he'd made to not care about a woman ever again. At that moment, he wanted nothing more than to make the world right for both Judith and Anna. He shifted closer to Judith and wrapped his arm about her shoulders.

She leaned into him, one arm about Anna.

Gil put his free arm over hers so together they sheltered the baby protectively. "We'll make sure it's enough."

"Believe me, sometimes one's best is not enough." She jerked away and hurriedly stowed the meal things. Done that, she reached for Anna. "You might as well rest. I can hold her as well as you can."

Feeling dismissed, Gil stretched out under the wagon, pulled his hat over his eyes and pretended to sleep.

He should have known better than to open his heart even a fraction of an inch. It wasn't worth the risk of being hurt and rejected.

He turned his thoughts to prayer. *Lord God, make Anna okay. Show us how to help her. Show us how to love—*

Was love worth the risk? It wasn't Anna he thought of. It was Judith.

Forgetting his own momentary pain at the way she pushed away when he offered his comfort, he let his mind return to the scene. *Sometimes one's best is not enough.* She'd spoken the words with the sureness of someone speaking from experience. He wished he'd pulled her back to his chest and asked her what she meant.

Maybe his prayer should change to asking to understand Judith.

He still mused over the scene when Buck called for them to move on. He sprang to his feet. Judith lay curled up on the ground, Anna sprawled beside her.

Judith sat up. "She's still sleeping." She gave the little girl water. Gil wanted to stay and do what he could to help, but it didn't take two to hold the cup to Anna's lips and he had to take care of the mules.

Ready to leave, he picked up the sleeping baby and waited for Judith to decide if she wanted to ride in the back or on the seat beside him. He admitted to a bit of pleasure when she chose the latter.

"Maybe Anna will wake up to watch the mules," Judith said, as she climbed to the bench.

Gil handed the baby up to her. His pleasure remained even if Judith's reason for sitting there had nothing to do with him. He climbed aboard and they moved onward. He tried to think how to ask her about what she'd said. Had her fiancé died despite her efforts to nurse him to health? He could guess how devastating that would be. When it wasn't certain if Stu would live or die he had experienced a dark feeling like nothing he'd before known.

They rattled over the prairie. Anna snuffled and rearranged herself but she did not waken.

Judith look's informed Gil of her worry. "It's not natural."

"Perhaps it's God's way of allowing her to adjust to the changes in her life." He had to believe in a good reason behind the behavior.

"I hope you're right." Judith stared at the mules, seemingly lost in thought.

He couldn't deny his curiosity laced with concern. "What did your fiancé die of?" He hoped his quietly spoken question wouldn't distress her.

She shuddered. "He wasn't ill."

He digested this information. "He had an accident?" He thought of Stu and how horrible it had been to see his suffering and wrapped his hand around Judith's.

"It wasn't an accident." She spat out each word.

"Then—?" The horror of the only other possibility churned his stomach. "He was murdered?" He couldn't get the words beyond a whisper.

She closed her eyes as if seeking strength. "Indirectly, yes."

"I'm sorry. I don't understand what you mean." How could someone be indirectly murdered? That was like almost being alive.

Her expression flat, she began to speak. "Someone

cheated Frank out of money leaving him defeated beyond recovery."

Gil turned the words over and over in his head. Defeated beyond recovery. What did that mean? He couldn't come up with an answer. "What happens when a person is defeated beyond recovery?"

"They quit living."

Her meaning became shockingly clear. "He ended his life?" He held back a dozen protests. Surely a man could recover from financial loss. Surely there were other reasons to live. Like a woman who loved him. That's what Judith meant when she said, *sometimes one's best is not enough.* She meant her fiancé had not found her best reason enough to live.

Acid burned up his throat. What an awful thought to leave her to struggle with. "I'm so sorry," he said.

"The official report is he died from fumes when the chimney didn't draw, but I overheard the sheriff tell my father that the chimney had been deliberately blocked."

He guessed she tried to sound cold, matter of fact, but the tremor in her voice betrayed the depths of her feelings. Lillian's unfaithfulness was a shadow compared to the unfaithfulness of this Frank. He could think of no other way to describe it. Shouldn't her beau have thought more of her feelings and less of his? Before he could find words to express his feelings, she sat Anna upright.

"I will not let this little girl give up on life."

Anna leaned her head back against Judith and continued to sleep.

"Maybe she's that tired. We don't know how long she wandered about lost before you found her and then she didn't sleep."

"Mrs. Shepton thinks she wasn't yet weaned so she's had to adjust to that as well." Judith looked at him with heartache in her eyes "Am I being harsh with her as an overreaction to what Frank did?"

"I think you are understandably concerned and I find that admirable."

Her gaze clung to his, seeking truth and strength. He offered both, ignoring the slightly mocking voice suggesting he imagined more than he saw.

"Thank you," she murmured. "So you think it's okay to let her sleep as much as she wants?"

He didn't know how much was too much. Most of all, he didn't want to voice his greatest worry—that this sleepiness was a precursor to the diphtheria.

Judith's eyes narrowed. "You're thinking she might be getting sick, aren't you?"

"I'm thinking it might be a possibility that's all. I hope and pray it isn't."

She drew in such a long breath he wondered if her lungs had no bottom. "If she is ill it would be unkind of us to try and waken her. I have been wrong to judge her to be like Frank." She shifted Anna so she lay cradled in her arms and rocking her, she crooned a wordless lullaby.

Gil caught the glisten of a silvery tear trailing

down Judith's cheek and rubbed her back. "Don't condemn yourself."

She faced him, the tears making twin tracks down her face. "I failed Frank. I will not fail Anna."

He pulled her head to his shoulder, wanting to croon lullabies and comfort to her. "You are not to blame for Frank's choices."

"How can you know that?"

He tried to think of a way to make her understand without speaking evil of the dead. "Because I have seen your loving, kind nature. You would have helped Frank if he had let you. I know that."

She held Anna safe with one hand and clutched at his shirt front with her other. A sob shook her shoulders.

"Did I say something wrong?"

She rocked her head back and forth and managed to speak. "You said exactly what I needed you to say. I wanted to help him. I tried to tell him money didn't matter to me. But I wasn't enough for him,"

"He was mistaken."

She clung to him and he held her as firmly as he could while guiding the mules. If the animals had been anything but well trained, he wouldn't have been able to hold her at all.

A moment later, she sniffed and sat up, adjusting Anna to a more comfortable position. The little one stirred and sighed but did not waken.

Judith and Gil looked at each other, sharing a mutual concern for the baby.

JUDITH MET GIL'S EYES. The man—her husband, she thought with a start of surprise—had offered her words of comfort that no one else had. Everyone pretended Frank had died in an unfortunate accident so they couldn't address how inadequate she felt at being deliberately left behind to handle all the raw emotions on her own. Frank had left her to do that. Her friends and family had forced her to continue to do it by not acknowledging the pain of how he'd died.

She feared that Anna would die—either from diphtheria or a broken heart. "No matter what, she will know love."

Gil's gaze echoed her vow. "Do you know the love chapter?"

She knew what he meant. "First Corinthians chapter thirteen. It's one of the passages Mama had me memorize when I had a broken leg."

"Say it for me." His smile melted a layer of hardness from around her heart and she quoted the chapter for him.

"Say again the part about what charity is like."

"' Beareth all things, believeth all things, hopeth all things, endureth all things.'"

"That is what love looks like." His warm gaze brushed a tender spot in her heart. "Perfect love comes from God, but we can offer that love to others."

She nodded. "If only Frank had believed that."

"If only Lillian had."

They silently acknowledged the truth and the pain of their confessions.

Gil took her hand. "We can do our utmost to do things differently."

She didn't know if he meant in regards to Anna or as man and wife and it didn't matter because she meant to apply it to both areas in her life.

The afternoon passed quickly as Gil pointed out aspects of the landscape that she might have missed. The different grasses—foxtail and goatgrass. She thought the flowers were all dormant for the winter but he pointed out some shy white asters near the trail.

The conversation shifted to talk of their childhoods.

"I spent many hours in my father's store," Gil said. "I made toys out of bolts and nuts. I made farms with them. Pa was patient with finding them lined up behind the barrels when he swept the floor. Rope made great corrals but Pa wouldn't let me take the new rope down. Instead, he gave me an old hunk of rope and said it was mine. I untwisted it so I ended up with many strands." He paused as if lost in his memories.

Judith enjoyed hearing how he coped as a mother-less little boy.

He continued. "One time someone left a bunch of pups to give away. Oh, how I begged Pa to let me keep one but he said no. A dog didn't belong in a store. I didn't let him see me cry when the last one was taken to a new home." He chuckled at the memory, but Judith saw a lonely boy sorely in need of a home and family.

"No wonder you were so happy to get a new mother."

"And a brother. I looked up to Ollie. He seemed to know so much more about life than I did. I don't know if he was all that pleased to have to share his mother, but he tolerated me and allowed me to tag along when he went places."

The wagon wheels turned round and round as they talked.

By the time the nearby wagons circled Judith had learned a great deal about Gil and likely he'd learned as much about her.

They stopped and Gil took Anna from her arms. He tried to wake her. She opened her eyes at his prodding, but her gaze remained unfocused and she couldn't hold her head up.

Judith saw her concern reflected in Gil's eyes.

"We can only wait for this to pass," he said. "I'll put her on the blanket and watch her while you gather the fuel."

She grimaced, although she was almost glad to have her thoughts diverted from worry about Anna. They couldn't be sure this would pass. "I'd forgotten about that."

"Kick the chips before you pick them up. That will scare away any critters."

"I'm not going out there unarmed." She reached for the shovel and stared at Gil as he roared with laughter.

"I thought we were going to take a gun," he said, when he could speak.

"I think I'll get more satisfaction out of whacking anything that threatens me." She marched away, his laughter following her. The sound filled her heart with an unfamiliar feeling of joy.

Why unfamiliar, she asked herself? Frank had made her laugh every day. But this was different. Gil was different. He cared more about how she felt.

Judith ground to a halt. How could she be so disloyal to Frank's memory? He had been a good man who treated her well. Except taking his own life didn't fit into either category.

She must be faithful to Frank's memory and keep her goal in mind. Find Frank's stepbrother and inform him of his guilt in Frank's death.

She gathered her apron into a pouch and forced herself to pick up buffalo chips. Mary Mae, Donna Grace, Mrs. Shepton and young Polly did the same keeping a distance from Judith. It almost looked like fun as the four of them chatted together and laughed.

Mary Mae paused to wave at Judith and they all turned to wave and call a greeting.

Judith waved back then forced her attention to her task. She longed to be able to visit with them and make supper jointly, but it would be four more days before they were allowed to rejoin the others and then only if none of them got sick.

She hurriedly gathered chips, gritting her teeth each time she had to pick up one. Only the necessity of a hot meal, the promise of hot coffee and the urgency to get back to check on Anna enabled her to keep at the task. Her apron full, she sped back to the solitary camp and dumped her load on the ground.

Gil sat beside Anna who still slept.

How long could one little girl sleep? Unless she was sick?

Judith went to the pair and touched Anna's forehead. It was cool. She lifted her little dress and felt her stomach. Also cool. Judith checked for a rash. Nothing. She turned Anna over which made the child whine a protest. Again Judith checked for any sign of something amiss.

She sat back on her heels. "There's nothing wrong that I can see."

"That should be good news."

She chuckled softly. "I suppose it is."

Gil prepared the fire while she mixed up batter for biscuits and sliced strips of salt pork to fry. She checked the water level and decided there wasn't enough to soak beans. But someone had sent them a bit of cheese. She'd save that for Anna when she woke up.

"It's ready," she announced.

Gil took his plate of food and went to Anna's side. "Maybe the smell of food will waken her." He held it close to her nose and called her name. Anna did not wake up.

Gil covered her against the evening chill and returned to the fire. He held out his hands for Judith's which seemed to be his preferred way to say the blessing.

She held his hands, and let his prayer of faith and gratitude fill her with peace.

Later, she gave Anna more water and wakened her enough for her to go potty then put her in the wagon and covered her well.

Neither Judith nor Gil seemed in a hurry to end the evening. They sat huddled in blankets listening to the harmonica and watching the flicker of the smoky fire in the circle of wagons where the others lounged. Even after the last of the fire died down, the last lonely note of the mouth organ faded and the murmur of conversation ended, they sat side by side.

Judith couldn't say what Gil's reason were for sitting up. She told herself she didn't want to go to bed because she worried about Anna.

Maybe, she thought with a gulp of guilt, Gil waited for her to leave so he could go to bed.

"It's late." Her cheeks burned as she scurried for the back of the wagon.

As she climbed in and pulled the canvas closer tight, she heard his soft reply. "No need to rush away."

No need to linger either, she silently answered as she settled in beside Anna. *Please, God, let her be okay. And please, please help her wake up. It really frightens me that she sleeps so long.*

What if she had the diphtheria?

What had Gil said? *Sufficient to the day is the evil thereof.* She knew what the saying meant. There were enough problems in every day without borrowing more from the future.

The sound of Gil settling for the night made her feel safe and sheltered and she fell asleep.

She woke to an unfamiliar sound. Like running water. Or a bubbling pot. She lay still trying to place the sound. Then it hit her and she sat up. "Anna, you're awake." She could barely make out the baby in the darkness of night, but there was no mistaking she was the source of the sound.

Judith pushed aside her covers, ignoring the cold air. What were they doing out in the midst of nowhere this late in the season? She rushed to the back of the wagon and loosened the ropes. "Gil," she called softly. "Gil." Already the black sky turned to gunmetal gray.

His hair tossed up, his eyes bleary, he rushed to the back of the wagon. "What's wrong?"

"Nothing." She touched his shoulder. "Listen."

He turned toward the prairie.

"No, in here. It's Anna."

He swung over the tailgate. "Is she—?"

"Listen."

He did. "She sounds happy."

"She's awake and happy and healthy and I'm so pleased." She hugged Gil.

He hugged her back. "I can't think of better news."

Thin light filled the air. At the main camp, men stirred.

"Anna is better," Gil yelled out.

A cheer went up from the camp.

Judith and Gil sat side by side, as the light grew, watching a baby who babbled and gurgled.

Buck rode close. "It's good news, folks, but we need to be on our way. I want to reach the river today."

Gil lifted Anna from the wagon.

Judith was so pleased with life, she didn't even mind building a fire with the buffalo chips though they did not burn at all like wood. While she made breakfast and Gil prepared the mules for their day in harness, Anna toddled about interested in everything from the spokes on the wagon to the rocks on the ground.

Gil returned and stood at Judith's side as they both watched the little girl.

"It is good to see her like this," Gil said.

"Indeed it is." He draped an arm across her shoulders and she wrapped an arm about his waist as they rejoiced together over Anna's improvement.

"I guess she was simply tired," he said.

"And sad. Sadness can make us do strange things."

He tilted his head to rest on her hair. "I'd say a good long sleep is one of the better ways of dealing with sorrow."

They laughed together then he asked the blessing and they ate breakfast. Gil and Judith laughed again as Anna went from one to the other demanding food from their plates. She consumed a great deal of food for one small body.

It was time to leave and they scurried around putting away the pots and pans. Judith offered Gil the last of the coffee. As he went to pick up Anna, she laughed and ran from him.

With a shout of joy, he chased her pretending she outran him.

Judith watched the pair, enjoying the way they both laughed.

He swept Anna off her feet and into a wide arc. Anna giggled.

Judith laughed too. Was there anything more beautiful than the sound of a baby's belly laugh? Unless it was hearing a man's deep, rumbling chuckle accompanying it.

Not until they were seated in the wagon and on their way did Gil remind Judith of something she had forgotten.

"Today is Sunday."

"Why, so it is." She looked longingly toward the other wagons. "They'll have a service tonight. Reverend Shepton will give a few words of exhortation or encouragement. How I wish we could join them and share our joy over Anna's improvement."

"We'll be able to hear them sing."

"Of course."

"We could have our own service. What would you think of that?"

"I didn't know you were a preacher too." She pretended both surprise and interest.

His eyes flashed. "I am a man of many talents, but preaching isn't one of them."

She longed to ask him to list his many talents but her tongue refused to work when she saw the teasing look in his eyes. "Then how will we have a service?"

"We can certainly rejoice over this little one." He indicated Anna who sat at their feet amused by her collection of rocks. "You could recite one of the passages you memorized. There must be one for happy occasions."

"I like that idea." Psalm Ninety-Six would be perfect. It was full of references to joy. She mentally rehearsed the verses as they rolled across the prairie.

They stopped for noon then Buck hurried them on. Shortly afterwards they reached a ravine. Judith and Gil remained at the rear as the other wagons crossed ahead of them.

Gil stood in the wagon, his hat pushed back. "I should be there guiding them down."

"There are plenty of experienced men. I believe I heard you say that."

"I know, but I feel so helpless standing here doing nothing. It's a steep descent and a man has to know how to approach it to prevent the wagons from tipping sideways or running away. I could tell them."

One by one the wagons crossed. The lighter wagons of the passengers went first and then the freight wagons. She knew the drivers of her brothers' wagons and held her breath as they headed down the slope. With much yelling they made it safely down and up the other side.

She knew by the way Gil curled his fists and mumbled instructions that the next three wagons were his. One of the wagons slid precariously at the edge, threatening to tip.

Gil leapt to the ground and took two strides forward.

Buck seemed to have anticipated what Gil would do and rode his horse between Gil and the wagons. "You cannot help." His order was loud and clear and Gil skidded to a halt. He planted his fists on his hips and took a wide stance as he watched.

The driver straightened the wagon and it rumbled down the slope and up the other side.

Gil visibly relaxed, but he remained watchful as the rest of the wagons crossed.

Buck waved to Gil. "Now you can go."

Gil returned to the wagon. "Take Anna on your knee and hold her tight."

Judith half expected the little girl to complain, but she played with Judith's fingers. Holding the baby made it impossible for Judith to clutch the seat so she settled for gritting her teeth and holding her breath as they began the descent.

Gil's entire attention was on guiding the wagon down the slope. The mules leaned back into the harness to keep from being pushed off their feet and then they were at the bottom. They passed the shattered remains of a recent crash then began the ascent.

"That wasn't so bad," she said, as they reached the top.

Gil laughed. "I could hear your teeth crack from the pressure you put on them."

"You could not." Then, realizing he teased her, she laughed.

They were several hundred yards behind the other wagons and eating their dust so he pulled to the side of the trail and increased the pace until they drew abreast of the lighter wagons, although they remained a hundred yards to the left of them.

The women waved to Judith and she waved back. Anna waved and called out.

"It sounds like she's saying hello." Judith laughed. "What a joy to have her like this."

Gil's smile warmed her clear through.

Judith could not stop a laugh from bubbling up inside her.

Gil quirked his eyebrows to ask what she found amusing.

"After the worry of the last few days, to have Anna well and happy just feels so good." Judith was content with this moment in her life. But she must not forget her purpose of this trip. It hadn't been to gain a husband and a child though she now had both and they would be a part of her future plans, but she would not, could not allow them to interfere with her quest to find Frank's brother. She was about to ask Gil if he knew of a Mr. Jones, first name unknown, a freighter on the Santa Fe Trail when Buck signaled for the wagons to turn off the trail toward the south.

The freighters grumbled, their complaints loud, as they forced the oxen to leave the well-marked ruts.

Judith knew it was unusual and leaned far to the right wondering why Buck had called for this action.

Smoke rose from a hollow a distance from the trial, ahead of them and on the north side. From that direction came the smell of burning wood and canvas and another scent that shivered up and down her spine. She tried to place the smell. It was familiar, yet not. The fire must signal danger for Buck to order them to skirt it. She shuddered though she couldn't say why.

"What's wrong? Why are we leaving the trail? " she asked Gil.

7

G il knew the reason for the smoke though he could not say who had started the fire nor if anyone survived the diphtheria. Perhaps the last person had set the wagons to burn before he perished. Whoever had done it had the good of others in mind. The burned remains of the wagons would inform anyone who came upon them to keep their distance. They'd realize the fire had been meant to kill a disease. Though there might be those who braved the threat in order to scavenge for anything useful. Both greed and desperation drove men to do strange things.

His insides twisted with regret over the death of so many people.

He reined in to let the other wagons swing away. They would keep a goodly distance from the burning wagons both to protect them from any contamination and to avoid the smoke.

"Gil?" Judith's voice reminded him of her question.

He shifted the reins to one palm so he could place his other over Judith's hand where it lay on her knee. "Remember I told you about the wagon train that was ahead of us?"

"Of course." Her gaze darted to Anna playing contentedly. "You found they had the diphtheria." Her eyes widened as she understood and she turned her palm to his and intertwined their fingers. "Oh, Gil. How awful." A tear clung to the lashes of each eye.

He wanted to wipe away that moisture but she held one hand and the mules required he hold their reins in his other. But her sorrow was his undoing. He could not ignore it and leaned forward to kiss each eye and capture her tears with his lips.

She leaned into him, her sadness gripping his throat.

Buck sat astride his horse waiting for Gil to follow the wagons.

Gil slipped his hand free of Judith's grasp but kept his head angled toward her. When she lay her head on his shoulder, he pressed his cheek to her hair and kept it there as they rejoined the wagon train, keeping to the left of them. Seeing the smoke from the fire of burning wagons reminded him of their own danger. *Lord God, healer and defender, protect us from that dreadful disease.*

After a bit, Judith sat up. "Why does anyone venture along the trail when the risks are so great?"

He could ask her what was so important that she

had begun this journey. Surely anything she needed to say or give to her fiancé's stepbrother could have been done through the mail. But now was not the time to point that out.

"Everyone has their own reason. For some it's need of money. Or adventure. For others, it's greed. For some, it's to escape a life that has grown unbearable. For others, it's the hope of finding something that's missing in their present life."

She shifted so she could look at him.

He held her gaze, hoping she would find comfort and encouragement.

"Gil, what really brought you on the trail?"

"I've already told you my story. After Lillian's unfaithfulness I wanted to get away. Pa and I had always known there was money to be made by trading goods into the Southwest. And I realized how much Pa needed the money. That's about it."

"Did you ever manage to pay off your father's loans?"

He shook his head. "He died before I could accomplish it."

"I know you give Stu money. Is that what compels you to go back and forth on the trail? There must be more to it than that. What else do you do with your earnings?"

Gil was a private person and had never told anyone what kept him going. But he found he had a need for her to understand him. "I support my mother."

"I thought your mother had died. Oh, you mean your stepmother. Does Ollie help too?"

Ollie! The man had taken all the money Pa and Gil had saved up and then disappeared. Maybe once or twice after he left, Ollie had contacted his mother to say that he was doing well. But Gil knew he had never sent any money. He'd assumed that had changed after he left home. Assumed Ollie sent money on a regular basis. To his shock after Pa died, he discovered Ollie had not sent money, but he had requested and received more, leaving Pa's business so far in debt that Gil had no choice but to sell it.

"I can't account for what Ollie does."

"You have three wagons, is that correct?"

"Yup." He could see Judith thinking through the logistics of three wagons, and two people to send money to.

"Are you saving money for something special?" Her gaze searched his thoughts, turned over rocks that he'd allowed to settle into place and exposed the truth.

"You remember me telling you how I used to play with the nuts and bolts in Pa's store?"

"Yes, didn't you say you pretended they were animals?"

"I think someday I might like to have a little ranch and raise cows and horses."

"And have your own dog?"

He laughed, but having her remember how much he'd wanted a puppy when he was a boy revealed another truth that he'd hidden. "Yes, I'd like a dog of my own."

"I hope your dreams come true."

"If they do, as my wife, you'll be a part of them." Another hidden truth made itself known. He'd always wanted a real home. "You and Anna."

Judith faced straight ahead.

He wondered if realizing that their futures were forever linked would bring her regret.

She leaned against the back rest and let out a long sigh. "I like the idea of a ranch. Like Luke and Donna Grace are planning."

Buck called for the noon stop and the chance to pursue this conversation passed as they hurried to do the chores and then he stretched out for a nap.

When they resumed the trip, Judith got into the back with Anna. "I think she might need a nap despite how much she slept yesterday."

They had been on the trail a little while when Gil glanced back. Anna lay in the crook of Judith's arm, two fingers in her mouth as she slept. From what he could see, he was quite certain Judith slept as well.

Gil settled in with his thoughts to keep him company. He'd grown good at limiting them to observations of his surroundings and awareness of what those around him did because it could affect the safety of the wagons, but now his mind wandered down long-forgotten paths. Did he want to give up freighting? Could he? He did a little mental arithmetic. With the money he made on this trip and what he had saved, he should have enough to take care of his stepmother and help Stu out. Perhaps even a little bit left to start a ranch.

Wouldn't he enjoy watching Anna helping care for calves and foals? He'd make sure she had a puppy and kittens.

The wagon train stopped. With a start, Gil realized they had reached the Little Arkansas and he'd let much of the afternoon slip by unnoticed.

Anna gurgled a happy sound as she and Judith came to the back of the seat. "We're stopped." Judith looked about as if searching for the reason. She saw the trees along the river. "We're at the Little Arkansas. No more buffalo chips."

He laughed. He stopped near the edge where he could see the proceedings. Again, he could do nothing but watch as Buck and the others dealt with the crossing. He stood, his hands curling and uncurling. The animals drank and the men filled the water barrels. Both men and women gathered fuel for the night. He did the same. Then the crossing began.

The mules struggled as they took the lighter wagons down the slippery, muddy banks across the narrow stream and up the other side. "They'll have to double up the teams to get the freight wagons across," he told Judith who had gotten down with Anna to let the child play.

"I know you would like to help."

"Yes." He kept his eyes on the bull whackers as they

unhitched and rehitched the teams. "It's a slow process but the only way to get across."

Judith sat on the short dry grass, her legs folded beside her. Anna ran from one interesting object to another.

"She's happy to be able to move about," Gil said.

"I'm happy to see her so lively."

"Me, too." He had forgotten to watch the wagons until he heard shouts and curses from the bull whackers driving the oxen up the far slope.

Gil held his breath until the wagon reached the safety of the far shore. The teams were unhitched and driven back to take over another wagon.

The sun had dipped toward the west before all the wagons had crossed. Gil followed the churned up trail with Judith and Anna beside him. The mules struggled in the mud and the wagon slipped from side to side but they soon reached the far side, safe and sound.

The other wagons had moved on despite the lateness of the day. Judith asked why.

"The grass here is poor but three miles further down the trail there will be decent grazing for the animals and they would need it after the last two days of poor rations."

"I'll be glad to have enough water for a decent wash and proper fuel for coffee."

"Are you trying to tell me you didn't enjoy walking across the prairies? I've always found them fascinating."

"And they might well be if one isn't picking up

buffalo chips. I never had time to look around. I was too busy making sure a snake didn't come slithering toward me."

He laughed and leaned closer to nudge her arm. "No snake would stand a chance against my well-armed wife." He'd meant to be teasing but when she slowly brought her gaze to his he wondered if he should have spoken those words.

Her gaze reached into his heart, seeking answers. He didn't know what her questions were and because of that, he couldn't know if he had the answers, but he let her search until she seemed satisfied.

She turned to look ahead. "It sounds like you have confidence in my ability to protect myself."

Her tone was neutral so he wondered if she liked believing that she needed no one or if she wanted to know his approval.

His answer came from the depths of his being. "I hope if you ever need me I will be there."

She nodded. "I hope you know I will always be here for you."

He reveled in her promise to be true and faithful. If only Lillian could have been so. But the pain of her unfaithfulness had lost its sting. He couldn't imagine her tromping across the prairie to pick up buffalo chips like Judith had done despite her fears.

Judith slowly came round to face him. "I wish Frank had realized that."

He understood she wanted Frank to have trusted her rather than end his life. How Gil longed to erase the pain that Frank's death had caused, but all he could do was what he'd just promised... be there when she needed him. Even if only to kill a snake.

The wagons circled ahead of them. The teamsters led the animals to water and then grass.

Gil stopped their wagon a hundred yards from the others. While he took the mules to graze, Judith built a fire and began food preparation.

She left pots bubbling and biscuits baking as they ate. He understood her plan to have extra food prepared for the next day. Their rations had been a little slim yesterday and he appreciated her efforts and told her so.

"It's my job."

"I know, but you do it well without complaining."

She chuckled. "With two older brothers I learned early in life the futility of complaining. Besides—" she gave him a steady look, "I take pride in doing my best at everything I put my hand to." Her eyes darkened.

He knew she again thought of Frank and how the way he ended his life convinced her he hadn't seen her as good enough.

"You certainly leave no room for complaint." It was far from adequate but the best he could find to offer her.

The meal was over, little Anna full and content. Gil tethered the mules close to the wagon while Judith cleaned up and tended the food still cooking.

By the time he returned, the harmonica played and

their traveling companions sang hymns of worship to honor the Sabbath.

He spread a blanket and he and Judith sat where they could watch and listen, Anna playing at their knees.

The music ended. Reverend Shepton rose. They could see him but not hear his words.

Gil turned to Judith. "Did you have a passage to recite?"

She looked into the distance. "I was going to say the Ninety-Six Psalm that speaks of God's glory and the honor and praise due His name but after seeing the smoke from those wagons—"

"Life is not always pleasant but God is faithful. We have many reasons to praise Him. Our own safety. Anna's health."

Hearing her name, Anna turned toward him. He cupped his hand over the back of her head. "That alone is enough reason for praise."

"You're right. I have to stop letting my thoughts grow dark and discouraged."

"I don't think you do, but of course you're troubled by the thought of what happened to those people."

"I'm ready." She sat up straight and fixed her gaze on him.

He did not blink nor turn away from her as she recited the Psalm, her voice growing strong and full, her eyes increasingly flooding with joy with every successive word.

A holy silence encircled them as she finished. He felt as if he breathed anointed air.

"I like the thought of the heavens rejoicing, and the fields being joyful. I will think of that every time I look at the trees, or the sky and the prairie. We should end in prayer." He reached for her hands and spoke of his gratitude from a full heart.

Darkness had enclosed them. Anna slept by their knees.

Gil carried the baby to the wagon and settled her on the bedding. She gave a muffled sound then curled to her side and sucked her fingers. He backed out. He didn't want to end the day but he must. The morning would come far too soon.

He helped Judith into the back "Good night," he said to her, and then spread his bedroll under the wagon.

They had three more days before the risk of diphtheria was over.

Would all three of them avoid getting the disease? Or would one or more of them deal with death and sorrow?

JUDITH RELAXED on the hard bed in the back of the wagon, Anna sleeping soundly beside her. The words of the Psalm and Gil's comments and prayer filled her mind with contentment. He was a good man. He was her husband. The latter still didn't seem real nor did she understand what it meant for her future. A ranch in the west sounded mighty nice. A home, a child and a husband who had confidence in her.

She didn't believe he would ever give up on life. Give up on her. In return, she silently vowed, she would never be unfaithful to him.

It was all reassuring but still left her wondering how their relationship would appear in the weeks and months ahead of them. He'd kissed her cheeks, had pulled her close. She had leaned into his arms, rested her head against his shoulder. It was pleasant enough. But did he want more? Did she?

Judith fell asleep with questions unanswered and woke with them pushed to the back of her mind. She heard Gil leave his place of rest and go to the mules. She hurried to dress Anna and slipped from the wagon. The coffee pot soon hung on the hook over the fire. Oats boiled in a pot. A large pan held potatoes… enough for breakfast and for eating cold for lunch. Pinto beans simmered and salt pork sizzled.

She leaned back on her heels and watched Gil bring in the mules and harness them. A good man, she repeated in her heart.

He swept Anna into his arms as he left the mules and came to breakfast. He settled Anna at his knees and took one of the baby's hands and reached for Judith's hand.

She took his and ducked her head, knowing he would think she bowed for prayer when, in reality, her thoughts and questions of last night and this morning made her self-conscious before him. With a guilty start, she realized that she'd been so busy thinking of her role as Gil's wife and what a future shared with him might look, that she'd let her reason for being on the trail fade. It was time to correct that mistake.

"Do you know of a Mr. Jones, a freighter on the Santa Fe Trail?"

"What's his first name?"

"I don't know."

"Jones is a common name but the only Jones that comes to mind is a wizened up old man who traps in the area. Don't know that he's ever freighted. Why do you ask?"

"My fiance's name was Frank Jones. I'm trying to find his stepbrother. I must find him." She rubbed at the tightness in her jaw, realized she'd gritted her teeth and forced the muscles to relax.

"And he's a freighter?"

"That's what Frank said."

"Sorry I can't help you on that matter. Perhaps when we get to Bent's Fort someone will know of this person."

She felt his study but kept her attention on her plate. What would he do? Say? If her search took her in a different direction than the one Gil meant to go? She'd promised to be faithful, but she'd also vowed to find the stepbrother and inform him how his actions had led to Frank's death. Gil would simply have to accept that she would return to him once she'd finished the task she'd set before her.

"Why is it so important to find this Mr. Jones?"

"There is something I must tell him." She continued to keep her gaze anywhere but on Gil.

"Hmm."

His quiet tone made her forget she meant not to look at him and she jerked her gaze to him and immediately wished she hadn't. His eyes filled with questions, and demands.

She could not break from his look as he spoke. "What happens if you don't find him? Do you plan to travel back and forth on the trail or go to every little settlement nearby until you do?" He didn't wait for her answer. "If I recall, you have promised me you would be faithful."

The accusation—for she knew it to be that—hung in the air between them. She sought for a way to make him understand that she could finish her task and rejoin him if he didn't wish to help her. "You could help me find him."

He studied her for a long, hard moment. She wanted to look away from the challenge in his eyes but would not. He needed to understand how much this meant to her.

His eyelids flickered. "It sounds like a wild goose chase. You don't know enough about him to have any hope of finding him." His expression hardened. "You have a husband and child now. That changes things."

She rose and made a lot of clatter as she gathered up the dishes to clean, stirred the beans and prepared them for travel.

Gil waited a moment as if he expected her to inform him that she was prepared to set aside her plans.

She couldn't. Until Frank's brother understood what his actions had done, Judith alone bore the silent guilt of Frank's death. How could she hope to live a happy, peaceful life with that burden?

It was time to get on the trail. She considered riding in the back, but decided against it. Gil might see it as evidence of a warring conscience when she wanted only for him to realize that she had not, and would not, change her mind. Somehow she must make him understand why it mattered. So she sat on the bench beside him, waved to her friends then settled in for another day of travel.

For some time, neither of them spoke. Anna's baby chatter filled the silence.

She sought for a way to explain why she must find Frank's stepbrother. Did her motives sound vengeful? Misguided? She didn't know. She only knew what she felt. Before she could adequately sort out her thoughts, Gil spoke.

"Are you regretting our agreement? I thought we were doing all right together."

She understood him to mean their marriage. "We are and I'm not regretting anything, but you must understand I ventured out on this journey for a reason and I can't abandon it."

"I'm trying to understand what is so important that you would travel a thousand miles in a wagon train to find a man whose name you don't know and nor do you have any idea where to find him."

It burned Judith's insides to hear him talk about her decision as if she was foolish. Silly. Worthless. Wasn't that what Frank had thought? "Frank thought me foolish and inconsequential. Not worth living for. Or fighting for." She tried to sound brave but heard the way her voice shook and hoped Gil wouldn't notice.

"Judith, I am not saying you are foolish. Simply that given how little you know, your plan is impossible."

"Seems to me that's what many people said about venturing out on these trails whether the Oregon Trail or the Santa Fe Trail. And yet here we are. And thousands of others."

He sighed. "What is so important about this man that nothing else matters?"

She hadn't said nothing else mattered, but that was how he interpreted it. "If you must know, Frank's stepbrother stole his money and left him with a failing business and so many debts he felt he could never clear his name. So he ended his life." Her words rushed forth, heated and uncensored. "Have you any idea how it feels to watch someone you care about struggle under such a weight? To see them lose heart and then know you aren't enough for that person to fight, to overcome his problems. To live." Breathless, she couldn't go on.

Gil didn't speak for a moment. "I might know a little about how it feels,but I still don't understand what you hope to gain by finding his stepbrother. Do you expect the man to pay Frank's debts?"

"I just want him to acknowledge his guilt in Frank's death so it isn't just me." Each word pushed past her teeth.

"I see." Gil's words were barely audible.

"I doubt you do." In desperation she edged forward on the seat and turned to face him. "Help me find him and then I'll never ask another thing from you."

His gaze held hers in a vise. She knew before he answered that he would refuse her request and sat back to stare straight ahead, seeing nothing but the darkness of her despair.

"Judith, if I thought it possible to find this man, I would accompany you, but I see it only as a waste of time and money.

"Fine. I understand." She wasn't worth the time and money the search would require. She shouldn't be surprised and she wasn't. After what Frank did she knew she wasn't worth any sacrifice whether great or small.

Why had she let herself think otherwise just because Gil was a good man?

8

G il kept his attention on guiding the mules along. Thankfully they required little help from him as they followed beside the other wagons.

He'd let himself be lulled into thinking and dreaming of a future with Judith. He'd even begun to think of leaving freighting and guiding to begin a new life with a home and family.

Were all women so ready to forget their promise of faithfulness or simply the ones he let himself care about?

But she couldn't walk away. There was young Anna to think of.

A dreadful idea slammed into his brain. Would Judith insist on taking Anna with her? He picked up the baby and perched her on his knee. "Anna is my responsibility. I promised her father to give her a home."

Judith shrugged. "How are you going to look after her on your own?"

"I'll hire a nurse, a nanny, a housekeeper—whatever the woman wants to call herself."

"Wouldn't it be easier to help me? That way we could stay together?" Her soft words beckoned.

She didn't realize how impossible it would be to find the man she sought, but Gil didn't want to spend their days divided on the subject. Given time she would come to a reasonable conclusion on her own. "I'll give it some consideration."

"Thank you."

Guilt stung his thoughts and brought heat to his cheeks. She trusted him to think about a matter that he had already made up his mind on. But it was the best he could do.

Anna pointed at the mules and babbled. Gil again told her the mules' names and made up stories about them, but after a bit Anna lost interest and squirmed to get down.

The other women walked beside the wagons.

Judith looked longingly at them.

"Two more days and we'll know if we've escaped the diphtheria," he said, hoping to make her feel better.

Air eased from her lungs. "Thinking about that makes everything else seem a minor detail."

"Indeed." Already she was seeing what mattered and what didn't. Soon she'd realize that finding Frank's stepbrother fit into the latter category. "Do you want to walk?" He stopped the wagon and she got down and lifted Anna to the ground. Her gaze went to the other women. They waved at each other. It was all they could do until the waiting period for the disease was over.

There was still a chance one of them might get it. He felt fine. He watched Anna. Since her worrisome day of sleeping, she bounced about as healthy and happy as anyone could expect. His gaze followed Judith. Hadn't she seemed lethargic since arising this morning? Did her steps lag? Her shoulders sag?

In his determination to make her understand the futility and waste it would be to spend her life trying to find Frank's stepbrother, had he overlooked something far more important—her health?

Anna bent to examine something and Judith stopped to watch her.

Gil eased back on the reins, not wanting to get ahead of them.

Judith looked up, a question in her eyes.

"I'll stay close in case Anna tires and wants to ride," he called above the noise of the wheels grinding along and the pots and tools clattering with every step the mules took.

Judith nodded.

Anna moved on, a rock clutched in her little fist.

Gil chuckled. "We'll soon be weighted down with her rocks."

Judith laughed. Her eyes flashed at him across the dusty prairie, He felt a deep connection to this woman. He would have faith that they would work things out. That it wouldn't be like Lillian. Or even Pa.

Pa? He stared ahead. Why would he think things hadn't worked out with his father? Why would he think of him in the same instance as Lillian?

Judith caught the side of the wagon. "Gil, let us aboard."

He stopped the wagon. She handed Anna up and the child added some rocks to her collection.

Judith sat beside him. "Gil, what's wrong?"

"Pardon?" Why would she ask that? She couldn't have read his thoughts.

"You were laughing about Anna and then your face fell." She searched his face. "You aren't ill, are you?" She touched his brow, her fingers cool, filling him with a yearning to turn his face into her palm. Before he could act on his foolish thoughts, she brushed her hand over his arm. "Please don't get it." Her voice cracked.

She cared. Despite her talk of finding Frank's step-brother, she cared. Surely she wouldn't leave him to search for a man she didn't even have a full name for.

"I'm feeling just fine." Better than that. He felt jubilant.

"Then what happened?" She looked beyond him to see if there had been something out there. There was nothing to see but prairie and sky and she brought her gaze back to him.

He could drown in the concern he saw in her eyes. "I was thinking of my pa."

"It looked to be a painful thought." Her hand rested on his. "What's wrong?"

He wasn't sure what to tell her. It didn't seem right to confess to an unkind thought toward a man who had passed from this world to the next, but the weight of her hand freed his thoughts. "I watched you with Anna and thought how sure I was that things would work out." He sucked in a deep breath. "Not like it was with Lillian. Right on the heels of that thought came another." He swallowed hard and couldn't immediately go on. "Not like it was with Pa," he whispered. He sought Judith's gaze and something more. Understanding.

"He was unfaithful?" she asked, her voice soft with no condemnation.

"I didn't realize that was how I felt about him giving all our savings to Ollie. The thought sneaked in unexpectedly."

"I suppose your father dispensed the money in good faith. He couldn't know Ollie would fail in his venture."

Gil nodded, eager to have the disloyal thought explained away. "I know he did what he thought was right."

"Of course he did. Things simply didn't work out."

She made it so clear. Pa had not given away Gil's money. "He invested the money and the investment failed."

"That's right." She squeezed his hand.

Buck called for the wagons to stop for noon and

Gil fed and watered the mules while Judith got out the cold food.

Anna was so glad to be down that she ran about in circles squealing. The camp dog ran out a few yards and barked at her. Anna stopped and stared at the dog then headed toward him.

Warren called the dog back.

Anna whimpered. Gil took her hand and led her to Judith. "Are you hungry?"

Anna immediately forgot everything else and ate eagerly. Before Gil and Judith finished Anna's head fell forward and then she slipped sideways and lay sleeping.

Gil chuckled. "Appears the little miss is tired." He looked Judith's direction and his heart skipped a beat at the warmth in her eyes. Had his desires been granted? Did she see that her role as his wife and Anna's mother exceeded any need to find Frank's stepbrother?

Gil carried Anna to the wagon and settled her in the back then stretched out in the shade with his hat over his head to rest. He heard Judith stow their lunch things and was aware that she walked away from the wagon. He lifted his hat and watched her, decided she was in no danger and covered his face again.

He wakened when he heard the teamsters hollering at the oxen to get moving. The snap of the bullwhips crackled through the air. He scrambled to his feet, stretching and yawning. He glanced about, but didn't see Judith. He looked inside the wagon but she wasn't there either. Anna slept peacefully.

Pulling his hat lower to shield his eyes he searched the landscape. No sign of her. He turned to the other wagons, now moving slowly forward. He didn't see her with them and didn't expect she would risk infecting them.

Buck rode up, stopping a distance away. "Time to roll out."

"Have you see Judith?"

Buck laughed. "Married six days and you've lost your woman? Is that some sort of a record?"

"Last I saw of her, she'd gone that way." He pointed.

"I'll have a look." Buck rode away.

Gil stared after him, his heart beating sluggishly.

A moment later, Buck turned back.

Gil took a dozen steps toward him but stopped as Buck signaled for him to wait. Buck reined in and leaned over his saddle. "She's over there. Best you go see. I'll keep an eye on your wagon."

Gil hesitated. "Anna's asleep in the back but she won't likely waken." Settled that the baby was safe, he trotted in the direction Buck had gone. Running was not something he did much of and he felt a little awkward, but he ignored the discomfort and continued on.

The muscles in his leg protested and he realized the ground rose in one of those almost invisible prairie hills. His heart hammered as much from fear at what he'd find as from the exertion he put forth. The ground leveled off and he would have stopped to catch his breath but worry over Judith propelled him forward. And then he saw her leaning on a thick branch, little moans coming from her and he ran as he'd never run before.

He reached her side. "Judith?" He spoke tentatively when she took no notice of his arrival. She stared at the ground and he followed her look. A snake...or what remained of it. It had been beaten to a pulp. He could barely identify it as a rattler. He shook her. "Did it strike you?"

Her pupils were too large.

He shook her again, gently but insistently. "Judith, did the snake bite you?

Her eyes focused and she shuddered. "No. I didn't give him a chance."

Gil choked back laughter knowing she wouldn't see any amusement in her circumstances, but it tickled him no end to see her use her fear to drive her to action.

No wonder she was so disappointed in Frank. Rather than give up on life or any single challenge, this feisty woman would tackle the problem head on and not give up until she'd conquered it.

Which might serve her well when it came to snakes, but he feared where it would take her in her pursuit of another kind of snake—Frank's stepbrother.

He eased the hefty stick from her fingers, put an arm about her shoulders and turned her toward the wagon. "It's time to be moving."

By the time they'd climbed to the top of the slope her silent shock had given way a different sort of shock...one of excited chatter.

"I heard the snake before I saw him. He wasn't more'n ten feet away. But he didn't know how much I hate snakes. It was unfortunate for him, but fortunate for me that a tree branch lay at my feet. I grabbed it and before that snake could think to do anything, I whacked him across the head. No snake is going to bite me without having a fight on his hands." She snorted. "Snakes don't have hands. So I don't know what he has. But it doesn't matter. I whacked him and whacked him. And then I did it again just to be safe."

Gil knew she must have hit the snake fifty times or more. He waved Buck away and led Judith to the wagon. He guessed she wouldn't sleep with the excitement and fear coursing through her body but she needed to be in the back to watch Anna and he helped her inside.

He stuffed back his laughter as he climbed to the seat. As he expected, Judith was too churned up to sleep and crowded to the back of the seat.

She leaned over the tailgate. "I guess I taught that snake a lesson he won't soon forget."

Unable to contain his amusement any longer, he roared with laughter.

She squinted at him a moment and when he didn't stop laughing she swatted him lightly on the shoulder. "It wasn't funny."

"You beat the snake to a pulp, but you think he

might have learned a lesson he won't forget." Laughter mangled his words.

"Huh. Wish he could spread the word to all his relatives to watch out for me."

"Yes, indeed. A bulletin should go out to warn all snakes of the vengeance of Judith Trapper." He sobered. Combining his name with hers felt awkward and yet that's how it was.

She quieted and leaned over the back, resting her chin on her arms. "I surprised myself."

"How so."

"Last time I saw a snake I froze. And in my dreams, I can never move or call for help. Strange how that has changed." She turned her head to look at him. "Wonder why I've changed."

He answered before he could think. "Must be marriage to me." Her face was mere inches from his and he looked into eyes that were brown as mink fur and as bottomless as the clearest mountain lake he'd ever seen. He could almost see her thoughts and knew that, at that moment, she didn't mind being his wife.

Then a curtain closed her heart to him and he knew she had thought of Frank and his stepbrother.

If only she could let go of the idea of finding the man.

JUDITH BOUNCED BACK and forth between wanting to shout to the world that she'd killed a loathsome snake and wanting to hug Gil for no other reason than he had seen what she did to the snake. And maybe a little because he was a good man.

If only he would agree to help her find Frank's stepbrother. Not until she had done that could she feel free of the condemnation of Frank's death.

A little later Anna wakened and Gil stopped so she and Judith could climb out. They walked beside the wagon for a while though Anna didn't walk so much as meander from one thing to another while Judith carried a shovel and kept a close watch for snakes.

She ignored Gil's chuckles.

Anna soon wearied and wanted to be carried. Judith didn't go far with the child in her arms before she asked Gil to stop and let them climb up beside him.

"See any snakes that need to learn a lesson?" His innocent voice didn't fool her for one moment.

"NEWS MUST HAVE GOTTEN around by now." She spoke in a tone of dismissal.

He chuckled and she admitted how much pleasure it gave her to be able to make him laugh.

She jolted upright as she realized something about Frank. He liked to laugh, but he did not take well to teasing. All his amusement came from laughing at others. How had she never seen that before?

"Something wrong? Remembering the snake?"

"You could say that." She did not like what she had

discovered about herself and searched her memories, hoping she had never laughed at someone with their knowledge. To her shame, she could not be sure. Had she really been selfish and cruel? Or simply blinded by her love for Frank?

She further examined her feelings. Was it love she felt? Or did his attention flatter her? She didn't realize she'd groaned.

"Judith, are you okay?" Gil caught her chin and pulled her round to face him. He searched her eyes and looked at her cheeks. "You aren't sick, are you?"

"No, I feel fine."

He exhaled. "Good." Then his eyes narrowed. "So why did you groan?"

She couldn't tell him, couldn't admit to being so self-centered. Instead, she sought for another reason. "Isn't it getting cold all of a sudden?"

His quiet study of her informed her that he knew she was avoiding his question. Then he tipped his head as if to say he would allow her to do so. For now. He grinned. "By my reckoning we are well into November. Can't expect August heat."

"No, of course not." But the wind had picked up and had a bite to it. She reached in back for a sweater for Anna and a shawl for herself.

"Can I get you a coat?" she asked Gil.

"Got it here." He reached under the seat and pulled out his coat and slipped into it.

Still she felt the cold and pressed close to Gil. She

drew Anna between their feet. At least she was out of the wind as she played on the floor.

Gil wrapped an arm about her and pulled her close. "Better?"

"Yes, thanks." She might be able to kill a snake, but that didn't mean she objected to being cared for from time to time. To feeling valued. Which brought her full circle back to Frank. If he'd valued her he would have lived and found a way to overcome his problems.

Clouds scudded across the sky and covered the sun. The sky grew dark. Judith wished they would stop and make camp but they rumbled onward.

The cold and wind had both intensified by the time Buck ordered the wagons to circle.

While Gil took care of the animals, Judith, shivering, built a fire. Anna fussed from cold and hunger and Judith fed her before Gil returned. He had circled around their wagon twice as if looking for something.

As they ate, she asked, "I noticed you took longer than normal making sure the camp was safe. Are you worried about something?"

"We are in for a good soaker and I need to be extra vigilant."

She noted that he did not meet her eyes and was convinced there was something more than that, but if he had taken care of it she had no need to worry.

They ate hurriedly, feeling the dampness in the air.

Gil donned an oiled slicker that had a musty smell to it. "Best you and Anna get in the wagon."

She hurried to comply and paused at the gate. "Where will you be?"

"I'll be keeping an eye on things."

She was right. "You're worried about something."

Before he could answer, the heavens opened and the rain fell in sheets. He pulled his hat low. "Close everything up tight and stay away from the canvas."

She knew better than to start water wicking through the walls but still, it was nice for him to show some concern. She wrapped a blanket about Anna, letting her keep a handful of rocks to amuse herself with and then draped a blanket about her own shoulders.

The pounding rain make it impossible to hear Gil although she strained to locate him. She hoped he would find shelter.

The inside of the wagon filled with a cold mist and she held Anna closer. The baby relaxed and fell asleep. The best thing for her. She'd stay warm and dry.

She hadn't done much praying since Frank died but had learned its value again with Gil's example and she prayed for safety for all, both here and at the main wagon train. Verses she'd learned with her mother's help came to her and she silently recited them, finding comfort in God's unfailing promises.

Fatigue overcame her and she lay her head upon her pillow but her sleep was fractured by the sound of the rain beating on the canvas and the memory of her encounter with a snake. She jerked wide awake at an unfamiliar sound. It took her a moment to place it and when she did, she sat up, her heart pounding against her chest.

The mules were braying. Gill had said they were as good as any dog or man at guard duty.

What had upset them? She strained to hear Gil. Was he safe? A fearsome thought claimed every bit of her brain. What if those murdering robbers had followed them and discovered the lone wagon? In the pounding rain, no one would hear them if they took it upon themselves to rob and even murder the few occupants in the hope of finding something to steal.

"Gil," she whispered, even knowing he couldn't hear it. If indeed he was able.

She needed some form of protection. What happened to the sturdy stick she'd killed the snake with? Hadn't Gil carried it back to the wagon? Where did he put it? She mentally retraced the movements. He'd slipped it under the seat.

Unmindful of the rain, thankful it had slowed to a patter, she slipped silently from the covers and inched forward, loosened the ropes and reached through the opening to feel under the bench. Yes, it was there. She pulled it inside, closed the opening again and sat ready, the stick in hand. She could kill a snake and she sure could defend herself and Anna from intruders.

She perched on her knees and held her club with both hands, turning her head side to side, straining for any sound that would warn her of danger.

The mules continued their ear-searing racket, making it impossible to hear anything else.

A shot rang out. And then a second. The mules quieted. She was certain she heard them shuffling and stomping, still restless.

She heard a thud and then something banged into the side of the wagon. She gripped her club with both hands and held it aloft.

No one was getting into this wagon without a fight.

9

"Judith?"

She knew that voice. But just to be sure, she whispered, "Gil?"

"Yes."

She tossed aside her club, loosened the rope at the back opening and leaned out to wrap her arms about his neck. "You're safe? Praise God. I was so worried." Her words were half laugh, half sob.

"You're going to get all wet." He reached behind his head to grasp her hands. She knew he meant to pull her arms away and she tightened her hold.

It had stopped raining but water dripped from the soaked canvas plopping on her head and neck. Her arms and the front of her soaked up moisture from Gil's clothing. "I don't care." Her tears intermingled with the moisture dripping on her.

Instead of unwrapping her arms from his neck, he slipped his own around her and held on.

It was too dark to see him so she trailed her fingers over his face to make sure he truly was okay. The tip of her index finger reached his mouth and her heart overflowed with emotions. She leaned closer and found his lips with hers. She might have been embarrassed, might have drawn back, but he claimed his own kiss before she could pull away.

She pulled back, but she did not end the embrace. At the moment, she wondered if she would ever be able to let him go. "Gil, what happened out there?"

"Some wolves had been following us and I guess the rain gave them reason to try and steal some food."

"That's what the gunshots were?"

"Yes."

"I was so afraid it was those murdering thieves." Something thudded into the wagon and she shuddered. "What's that?"

"I tied the mules to the wagon. They're restless and upset and I didn't want them to run off on us."

"You're cold. Come inside with us."

He eased back. "I'm too wet."

"It's stopped raining but there'll be no dry place to lay your head. Take your slicker off and hang it on the side of the wagon. I won't feel safe unless you're where I can see you." And touch him.

"Buck has posted extra guards and I can hear the mules if anything upsets them."

She wondered if he was arguing with himself and decided to add her own thoughts to sway his mind. "There's plenty of room in here." Without any trunks or furniture, the inside was almost roomy.

When he continued to hesitate, she took his hat, shook the water from it and hung in on the end of the wagon.

He slowly slipped from his slicker as if he needed the delay to find an excuse to refuse her invitation. The smell of rain, wet canvas and nearby animals wafted to her. Clouds hung low, making it so dark she couldn't see anything but shapes.

As soon as the wet garment had been hung to drip, he bent to work his boots. When he straightened, she found his hand and gently urged him toward her, letting go only when he lifted one leg over the tailgate and swung inside.

She shifted to one side, Anna asleep at her feet and Gil sat beside her, his back to the tailgate. She reached out, searching for his hand. When she located it in the dark she clung to it. He turned his palm to hers and their fingers intertwined. Only then did she realize that it had been a long time since she'd properly filled her lungs and she sucked in the damp air.

She pawed about with one hand until she found the blankets, made sure Anna was well covered then pulled the others over herself and Gil.

Slowly, she felt him relax. "You must be tired. Go to sleep."

"I have to stay alert."

"Didn't you say Buck had posted enough guards?"

Just then a shot rang out and he started to rise.

She pulled him back. "Someone will let you know if you're needed." As if to prove her point Buck called from nearby. "Just another wolf. No need for concern."

"There you go."

He sank back beside her and tipped his head back but he sat up too high. He slid lower until he found a headrest. Within minutes, his head lolled to the side and rested on her shoulder and she knew he'd fallen asleep.

She eased downward hoping he would slip into a more comfortable position. His head jerked up and he moaned.

"It's okay," she murmured. "Go to sleep." And even though he wasn't a child, she hummed a lullaby.

He stretched out and she smiled, knowing he needed to rest and would have denied himself without a little urging from her.

The mules shifted about. The camp dog barked once and was ordered to be quiet. Anna snuffled in her sleep. Beside Judith, Gil breathed deeply. Once he called out something in his sleep, but she couldn't make out what it was.

A baby slept at her feet. A man—her husband—slept beside her. The dangers she feared had passed. The rain had stopped and the world outside the wagon was quiet.

All was right with her world.

GIL CAME AWAKE IN AN INSTANT, but lay motionless as he tried to think where he was and how he got there.

The dark shape of the canvas said he was in the wagon. Right. Judith had persuaded him to join her here last night. Not that it took much persuading especially after she'd kissed him. And he'd kissed her right back, finding her warm lips an enticing contrast to his own cold ones.

Judith curled into his side still slumbering, her body warm, and her breathing deep.

He should have refused to sleep in the wagon. Shouldn't he? But he could think of no cause. Judith was his wife. He had every reason to spend the night with her. Morning sounds reached him. Men yelling at the oxen, the rattle of harness and the crack of whips. The mules tethered to his wagon shuffled about, knowing it was time to get to work. Gil should slip away, but the temptation to stay where he was kept him from moving.

Anna stirred and sat up. "Mama." She crawled over and patted Judith's cheeks. "Mama."

Judith's eyes opened. "Hello, little girl. How are you?"

"Mama," Anna said.

Judith hugged Anna. "Yes, I'm your mama now."

Gil knew the moment she realized he lay beside her. Her breathing stalled. Slowly she came round to face him. Her eyes were sleep clouded.

"Good morning." His gaze drifted to her mouth. Would she allow him another kiss?

She blinked, sat up and looked around. "It's morning."

He sat up too, grinning at her. "So it is."

She pulled Anna to her lap and looked past him. "You stayed here the night."

"We are married," he felt compelled to point out, waiting and wishing for her to meet his gaze.

She shoved the blankets the rest of the way down. "I have to start breakfast." She tucked Anna under one arm and started to climb from the wagon.

"Wait. I'll give you a hand." He bolted to his feet, discovered he was in his socks then remembered he'd left his wet boots outside. He scrambled over the gate and worked his way into the shrinking leather. By the time he had them on his feet, Judith had gotten down under her own steam and went to build a fire.

She looked about for dry wood and found the store he had stuffed under the wagon. She continued to carry Anna in one arm, reluctant, he supposed, to put her down in the wet grass.

He lifted his slicker from the side of the wagon and spread it on the ground. "She can play here." He took Anna from Judith's grasp. His hand grazed her arms and her gaze came to his. At the uncertainty he saw, he touched her cheek.

"Judith." His heart filled with so many things—tenderness, longing, surprise at how much he wanted her to be part of his life, part of his plans. But not a word came to his mind.

She released Anna to his arms and returned to the task of building a fire.

He watched her a moment, wanting so much to ease the tension between them, but not knowing how. Perhaps it was best to simply continue on as they had. Or not. He simply didn't know. Seems spending four years on the Santa Fe Trail with mostly men and animals to deal with had robbed him of the ability to deal with his feelings.

After he settled Anna, he went to the animals. It was usually easy enough to think of nothing but feeding, watering and harnessing the mules. Most of his attention was normally occupied with studying his surroundings, being aware of every sound and movement, always alert for danger and change. But today was different. Although he tended the animals competently enough, and his gaze often scanned his surroundings, his thoughts circled around Judith and what to think of last night. She'd seemed awfully glad to see him. Had insisted he climb into the wagon. She'd seemed concerned that he be warm and dry, but this morning, she appeared to regret all that. He didn't know what to make of it.

He returned and took the cup of coffee she offered. "Thanks." He hunkered down by the fire, glad of the heat on the chilly morning.

"You can help yourself to the food. I want to finish feeding Anna."

"I'll wait and enjoy my coffee."

Judith offered Anna another spoonful, but the little girl refused more and toddled over to Gil. He perched the baby on his knee. She babbled about something but as usual he didn't understand what she said, but he followed Judith's example and nodded. "Yup. That's right. Sure thing."

Anna seemed to approve of his replies.

He glanced up in time to catch a smile on Judith's face.

"You better be careful what you're agreeing to," she said. "Isn't that what you told me?"

"Soon enough we'll have to watch what we agree to." He held her gaze, felt her questions and uncertainty. He smiled. "Agreement doesn't have to be something to avoid." He meant their marriage and hoped she'd understand his simple message that he didn't regret having taken this step even if she might have cause to think he had been forced into it.

"Sometimes we agree to things without knowing what we've agreed to." Her eyes begged for assurance. Or at least that's what he told himself. And knowing how Frank's manner of death had left her feeling uncertain he was pretty sure he had it right.

He put his cup down and closed the distance between them.

Her eyes narrowed. She glanced to her side as if wondering if she could escape.

He caught her by her shoulders. "I don't regret my choice."

She stared at him. Her gaze went to his mouth and he did the only thing he could think that would convince her. He lowered his head and caught her lips with his. He lingered, tasting coffee. His heart drank in her sweetness.

She leaned toward him as he ended the kiss and he chuckled.

"Papa," Anna tugged at the knee of his jeans.

"Papa, is it?" He laughed and swung Anna into the air.

He and Judith smiled at each other over Anna's head. "Seems she's adjusted to her new family."

Judith's smile faded. A darkness filled her eyes. Without her speaking he knew her thoughts had gone back to Frank's stepbrother who had robbed her of the husband and family she'd expected to have.

He knew he couldn't replace Frank in her affections, but couldn't they move forward from here, accepting Frank and Lillian as their past? Instead she clung to it, thought finding Frank's stepbrother would somehow make it more bearable. He didn't see how it would. Figured clinging to that notion made it impossible for her to embrace the present or look to the future.

Gil was part of the present and the future and as such didn't fit into her plans. Yet she had married him, promising to be faithful. That seemed to mean one thing to him and quite another to her.

BREAKFAST OVER, everything stowed for the day's journey, Judith sat beside Gil on the hard wooden seat, Anna playing at their feet.

So many things raced through her mind, tangling her thoughts until she couldn't sort out one idea from another. She'd been kissed by Gil, not once, but twice. She'd even initiated the first kiss which gave him cause to think she meant—what did she mean? She'd been glad to see him, to know he was safe and she was safe. Was that all the kiss was? Gratitude. She couldn't say. Or perhaps she didn't want to.

She had vowed to find Frank's stepbrother and if she abandoned her quest simply because something else had come up was she any better than Frank or his stepbrother? She didn't think so. A person should live up to their promises and responsibilities. She had to right the wrong between the brothers. Of course, she couldn't undo what was already done, but by getting the brother to acknowledge how his wrong doing had caused Frank to end his life, she felt she was somehow making it right for Frank. That had been her goal from the beginning, but now it didn't seem so simple because she'd also promised to be faithful to Gil and, as he had said this morning, she was now part of a family.

There was only one way to resolve her quandary and that was to get Gil to help her find the man she sought. She'd asked him directly, but now decided to come at it sideways.

"Do all the freighters go through Bent's Fort?"

"Bent's Fort is on the mountain route of the Santa Fe Trail. Lots of people choose the Cimarron Cut Off and miss Bent's Fort altogether."

"Oh." She did know that, but hadn't considered how it would impact her search. "But they all go to Santa Fe in the end?"

"Pretty much, unless they end up like the wagon train we saw back there."

She knew he referred to the one that carried the diphtheria. Frank's stepbrother might have passed through Bent's Fort, gone the Cimarron Cut Off or perished. That left a lot of territory for her to explore. "But if a freighter has been on the trail for a few years maybe someone at the Fort will remember him."

"Could be." Gil's voice hardened. "Or it could be this stepbrother has never been on the trail or is entirely made up."

She pursed her lips. "Are you accusing me of fabricating a story?"

"Just saying it's easy to blame someone with no name and no address for problems."

"You're calling Frank a liar."

"Just pointing out possibilities."

She slid as far from him as she could, pretending it was so she could retrieve one of Anna's rocks.

They rode in tense silence.

Buck called for them to stop for the noon meal.

She barely waited for the wheels to stop turning before she alighted and rushed back to the food larder to bring out the cold meal.

Gil put Anna on the ground and Judith fed her while Gil tended the animals and she ate her own meal before he returned.

She handed him his food. "Would you mind looking after Anna while I take a walk?"

"Better take your club in case you encounter a snake." He lifted her weapon of choice from the back and handed it to her. He grinned and she knew he teased her, wanting to end the tension between them, but she couldn't relax, and the smile she gave him probably looked as wooden as it felt.

With muttered thanks she strode away.

Why would Gil suggest that Frank had made up his brother? She went over everything she could remember of what Frank had said. He'd been quite specific in saying his brother freighted on the Santa Fe Trail. "Good way to make a fortune," he'd said with some force.

"I hear it's a rough life," she'd replied. "I can't see you liking it." Frank enjoyed his nice suits and hats. He would have snorted in disgust to see Gil's battered hat.

"You're right. I'd despise it. No. As soon as I get my shipment of goods, I'll make my money living in town." He brushed a fleck of dust from his suit.

Frank had talked about his shipment of goods for the six months she had known him. When she questioned him about how long it was taking, he laughed.

"All in good time. I'm happy enough to be a man of leisure at the moment." He'd smiled adoringly at her. His attention always made her feel special.

She looked at her dusty skirts. Frank would be shocked at her state. She had brought only one fine gown such as he'd think she should wear and she'd been married in it.

Married and vowed to be faithful. Not that she would ever be tempted to consort with another man. Yet another man drew her attention. Frank's stepbrother. That wasn't the same as being unfaithful. Not at all. Surely Gil understood that.

A picture of Gil came to her mind. Gil in his battered hat that protected him from the sun and rain. She recalled how she had taken it from his head last night.

And how she'd kissed him.

Frank's life of leisure had ground to a halt. He explained how his father owed him money and that was how he meant to buy his goods, but his stepbrother had taken the money for his own pursuits. Frank had been evicted from the store he rented and from the nice house where he and Judith planned to live. Even his fine horses had been taken by creditors.

Frank had retreated to the little rundown cabin on the property where he'd once rented pasture for his horses. And that was where he died.

Judith sank to the ground and bent over as pain crashed through her.

She hadn't heard Gil approach. Didn't know he

was there until he sat beside her and held her close. She wanted to lean into him and forget her past but she couldn't.

"No one can understand how awful it felt for me to be left with nothing but shattered dreams." It didn't matter whether or not he understood what she meant.

Thankfully, he didn't offer platitudes or try and convince her to forget her past. He simply held her.

The intensity of her pain passed, settling into the pit of her stomach. She knew from experience it would stay there, sometimes lulled into slumber, but springing to life at unexpected times.

Gil had brought Anna and lifted her to Judith's knees.

"Mama," Anna said.

Judith's eyes clouded with tears as she kissed the chubby neck. They were family as Gil had said. But even that could not heal the pain within. Only one thing could.

She must continue to look for Mr. Jones.

Tears slipped from her eyes and dampened her cheeks.

Anna looked concerned. Gil shifted the baby to his arms and wiped Judith's tears with his thumb. He got to his feet and offered Judith a hand. "The wagons are moving."

She allowed him to help her upright and then slipped free of his hand. He'd made his opinion clear about her intention of finding Frank's stepbrother. He thought it a foolish goose chase and perhaps even a fabrication.

If he wouldn't help her, he left her no choice but to continue looking on her own.

She had yet to figure out how to do that while remaining true to her promises to Gil and Anna to be wife and mother.

10

Gil's insides felt like they'd been torn by a dull knife as Judith pulled away from him. All his life, the one thing he'd longed for was someone who cared solely for him. His stepmother was the closest person to offer him that and he knew it was because he was all she had left. He admitted it wasn't that he wanted just anyone to care for him. He wanted his wife to care in that special way.

In all fairness, he'd entered into this relationship knowing neither of them expected or offered what he dreamed of. But in the last few days he'd hoped things had changed. Seems he'd put more importance on the value of a kiss than he should.

Her agony over Frank's death made him understand how wounded and broken she was. How she must have loved that man and yet he didn't care enough about her to live.

Judith said she would ride in the back with Anna. He wasn't surprised though he was disappointed when she didn't slip forward and lean over the back of the seat to talk to him. Last night meant nothing to her. Their kisses meant nothing to her.

He tried not to compare her to Lillian though in his heart, it felt the same. Judith was here. She rode in the same wagon. But her heart belonged to another.

Could they continue to live together, be father and mother to Anna and yet have this vast chasm between them?

The afternoon hours hung heavy about his shoulders. There was so much he wished he could say to Judith, but he didn't have the words and she didn't want to hear them even if he did.

A couple of hours later, Anna wakened and called, "Papa."

Gil would have rejoiced without reservation at being called that but it was impossible to be a hundred percent happy when he wondered what Judith would do. He knew she wanted him to help her find this man who might not even exist. If he agreed they might spend the next ten years searching up and down the trail and across the Southwest without finding him. That was not what he wanted in his life. Nor did he think it would be the best thing for Anna. Or Judith for that matter. He ached for a home to be shared with her and Anna. Not the restless sort of life he'd lived these last few years.

They expected to go on to Santa Fe but he doubted

the mountain pass would be open this late in the year. They might be forced to spend the winter at Bent's Fort. He had a few weeks before they reached the Fort. He could only hope and pray they would come to an agreement of sorts before that time...one that gave him the desire of his heart. All she had to do was give up this mad chase. Was that asking too much?

Anna patted him on the shoulder and babbled a demand. He might not understand her words, but he understood her message. She wanted to be up front with him. He was about to ask if he should stop when Judith lifted Anna over the back of the seat to the floor.

He couldn't continue this way. "Whoa." Old Brighty flicked his ears, as if wondering why they stopped while the other wagons continued on.

Gil turned in the seat. Judith sat at the back, her expression wary.

"I'm sorry," he said. "I didn't mean to suggest Frank was a liar nor to suggest his stepbrother doesn't exist. Can you forgive me so we can continue to be friends?"

Her eyes were dark and expressionless. She hid her thoughts from him.

"I have to find Frank's stepbrother."

"I don't understand why it's so important. What difference it will make."

"I know you don't understand and I don't expect you to. But he is partly to blame for Frank's death and I want him to know that."

"How will that change anything?"

She rocked her head back and forth as if frustrated at his lack of understanding.

"I'm trying to understand. Please help me."

She sucked in air. Her expression hardened. "It will make it not all my fault."

He jumped over the seat and knelt before her. "Judith, you know you aren't to blame for Frank's choices."

"I carry the guilt and will continue to do so until I can make his stepbrother admit his share."

He didn't understand and likely never would. "Aren't I and Anna enough reason for you to put the past behind you and look to the future? We are a family now and I would like us to find a little bit of land and have a real home. I thought you wanted the same thing."

"You're hurt because you don't think I see you as enough reason to forget my quest?"

"I admit I am."

"Then you know to a tiny degree how I feel to know I wasn't enough reason for Frank to face his future." Her voice dripped with sorrow and likely the guilt Frank's death had burdened her with.

He pulled her to his chest.

At first she resisted then softened in his arms. "I'd do anything I could to change what happened to you but it's impossible to go back and alter the past."

"I know you think I should forget it and move on but I can't." She pushed away and drew her knees up to her chest. "I can't until I find that man." Her voice grew strong, stubborn, and perhaps even desperate.

It seemed they would forever be divided on this matter. If not for Anna and her need for a real home, Gil might have decided to help Judith even though he knew how futile her search was. He'd been on the trail four years. He'd encountered dozens of other traders both on the trail and in the various forts and trading posts. Apart from the old trapper, he had not heard of a man with the name Jones—first or last name.

"Mama, Papa." Anna grinned at them over the back of the seat.

They were on their feet instantly, rushing forward to grab Anna lest she tumble off.

They both laughed as Gil scooped her into his arms.

"She's a little monkey," he said. "We're going to have to watch her more closely to make sure she doesn't get herself into trouble."

"I'll sit up front where I can keep an eye on her." Judith climbed out the back.

"Good move," Gil whispered to Anna. The baby had accomplished what Gil couldn't—Judith returning to her good nature and ready to sit beside him.

Gil handed Judith the little girl before he jumped over the back of the seat and took the reins. Determined to bring the mood to a better place, he told her stories of people and events he'd experienced on the trail.

He told her of the naturalist who had been with them last year. "His name was Dusty Leaf."

She laughed, the sound settling deep in her heart. "You sure you're not making that up?"

"That's what he told us and I had no reason to question his honesty."

"Really? Somehow I doubt that you'd let a name like that go without comment." The look she slanted his way said so many things—that she knew his bent toward challenging things and maybe even that she liked that characteristic.

"Okay, the truth? He said his name was Darwin Leaf but kids in school teased him and called him Dusty Leaf. He liked it so much he kept the name."

He told her of the many things Dusty had taught them about the prairie, the plants and the animals. "I have always found the prairies to have a special appeal, but I saw them differently after that."

Judith looked about. "One would think there is nothing to see but grass."

"You have to have eyes to see and ears to hear what's around you."

"I know and I am beginning to see and hear." The sweetness of her smile made him believe she'd forgotten Frank and his stepbrother for now.

"We're almost at Cow Creek. That's where we'll spend the night."

The long line of wagons turned aside from the trail and circled.

Gil chose a spot for their wagon close to some box

elder and hackberry trees that would provide a little protection from the weather which was hot at the moment, but he knew it could change at any moment.

The teamsters led the oxen and mules away to water and grass. A few horses were left tied to wagons to be cared for later.

Gil was about to take his mules to the creek when shouts and thudding horse hooves made him draw back into the trees.

Judith crowded to his side, Anna in her arms. "What is it?"

"Could be trouble." As if to confirm his words, gunfire filled the air. Raiders rode between the men and the wagons cutting off the men from returning to protect their possessions, the women and little Polly. The women screamed and men shouted.

Gil reached for his rifle. "They're being attacked. Stay here. Take Anna and hide in the trees. Keep her quiet." So far the men hadn't noticed the lone wagon nor would they expect return fire to come from behind them.

He edged away from the wagon, not wanting to bring shots in that direction. The teamsters had their hands full trying to keep the animals under control. Then a pair of mules raced along the creek and the rest of the herd followed.

"Let them go," Warren called. "Back to the wagons."

The intruders shot at the men forcing them to find shelter near the stream. Two of the raiders raced toward the wagons.

Gil knelt down, sheltered by the trees and took aim at the lead rider. He fired. The rider's horse reared back, the man had to fight to stay in his saddle.

At the same time, gunfire erupted from the wagons.

Gil got off another shot and another, smiling at how surprised the would-be robbers were to find themselves facing return fire from the women left at the wagons. Several men had stayed behind as well and they also fought off the intruders.

Three of the front-riding men turned away and yelled at the others to leave. Firing over their shoulders, their horses kicking up a cloud of dust, they rode away. The thunder of hooves faded. Gil waited to make sure they didn't circle and return then trotted toward the creek intending to help round up the animals.

Buck rode toward him. "We'll get them. You stay at your wagon. We won't know if it's safe for you to rejoin us until tomorrow."

Gil drew up. He'd forgotten about the diphtheria. "Someone should have known there were men nearby and recognized the danger," he called. He was sure he wouldn't have overlooked the possibility but he wasn't the scout right now.

Buck touched his finger to the brim of his hat and turned his attention to the task of rounding up the scattered animals.

Gil returned to the wagon where Judith and Anna waited. "I should be helping," he muttered. "What's more, if I was scouting we wouldn't have ridden into a trap."

Judith touched his arm. "They were driven off." She tented her hand over her eyes. "Was anyone hurt?"

Mary Mae stepped from the circle of wagons. "We're all okay," she called. "Are you?"

"We're fine," Judith raised her voice to be heard across the distance. They all looked the direction the animals had gone.

Feeling helpless, Gil took the mules to water, then brought them back and tethered them nearby to graze. He double checked the ropes. He had no intention of losing them and wasn't prepared to believe the marauders wouldn't return.

Judith built a fire and turned her attention to preparing the evening meal. The scent of baked beans and fried salt pork informed him the women at the wagon train were doing the same thing.

The men on foot returned, leaving the men on horseback to follow the animals and turn them back.

Gil hunkered down by the fire. Anna toddled to him. "Papa?" She held out her arms.

He picked her up. She pressed her head to his shoulder.

Judith watched them. "She senses that you are unhappy and wants to comfort you."

Gil hugged Anna. "Thank you, sweet child." He couldn't continue to feel bad with Anna hugging him. Only one thing would make him feel even better and he held out a hand to Judith.

She barely hesitated before she took his hand and allowed him to pull her to his side.

"I'm glad everyone is okay," she said.

"It could have been much worse." He turned the direction the animals had gone. "It might take some time to get the oxen and mules back." The sound of gunshots had sent them into a panic. He did not speak his worst fear that the raiders would drive the stock farther away and leave the wagon train stranded.

Judith must have sensed his worry. "You don't think it's over?"

"There were ten of them. Why did they give up so easily?"

She shivered. "They're waiting for dark."

He regretted that she knew this was his worry. "We will be on guard. There are a lot more of us than them." Which gave him even more concern. Why would they attack under those circumstances? The only answer did nothing to ease his tension. Because the only thing that made sense was they intended to drive the animals away and leave them stranded. The wagon train could stand off an attack for some time but they couldn't last forever. They would run out of food. And the worst was he and Judith and little Anna were alone. How could they withstand an attack? The only way was to remain out of sight in the shelter of the trees.

"Has the coffee boiled?" he asked.

"It should be ready by now." She went to fill his cup.

"No more fire." He grabbed the shovel and covered the flames with dirt until they died.

Her eyes widened with realization of why he'd done it. Anna played nearby and she grabbed the child. "How are we going to hide?"

"I don't know if they realized we were here." Though if they'd been following the wagon train, and it seemed likely they had, they would have noticed that one wagon kept a distance and camped apart.

Judith jostled Anna to keep her quiet. "It's six days. Can't we join the others?"

"Buck said one more day. We have to be sure." He touched Anna's forehead. "No sign of anything with her. None with me. How about you?"

Judith cleared her throat.

His heart squeezed hard. "Do you have a sore throat?" If she got the diphtheria they wouldn't be able to rejoin the wagon train but that was the least of his concerns. He did not want her to get sick. He did not want to lose her.

"I'M FINE," Judith said. She was sure they weren't going to get sick. They should be allowed to join the others. They were easy prey out here by themselves. Last night had taught her just how frightening it was to be so vulnerable. What if something happened to Gil? Losing Frank had taught her how awful it felt to lose someone she cared about. She did not want to repeat the experience and add to the pain she already bore.

"I'm not staying at the wagon tonight," she announced. "That will be the first thing they'd attack."

"My thoughts exactly. We'll eat and stay here until dark then we'll hide away from the wagon. I'll scout around to find a place, but I'll be sure to make it look like I am only checking on things like I always do." He squatted down by the now dead fire.

The last thing Judith cared about was supper, but thankfully some of the food she prepared was done and she served it to Gil and Anna.

"You must eat," Gil said.

Rather than argue, she took a small portion. Gil held out his hand and the three of them formed a circle with joined hands as Gil prayed.

"Lord God, You see all. You see these raiders. Foil their plans. Protect us. Keep us from getting the diphtheria. Protect all our friends. Help the men find the animals. Thank You for always being our Guide and Defender. Thank you for the food. Amen."

He released her hand and he and Anna began eating.

His prayer had comforted and given Judith courage and she slowly ate.

When he finished, he announced, "I'll make sure everything is safe for the night."

Did he speak for her benefit or did he think someone might be watching close enough to overhear them? She glanced over her shoulder, cold racing through her veins.

Gil brushed his hand across her shoulder as he passed. "Act casual," he murmured.

Anna took a step after him but Judith caught her and distracted her by showing her how to bounce a spoon on the palm of her hand and Anna laughed and wanted to see it again.

Judith strained over the baby's happy sounds for noises coming from the bushes. Gil had slipped away silently. Her heart pressed to her ribs and managed a sluggish beat. Without thinking her arms tightened around Anna until the baby squirmed.

How long had Gil been gone? It seemed an inordinately long time. She glanced over her shoulder toward the other wagons. What would they do if she ran into the sheltering circle to seek protection?

Judith sorely missed her friends and family but she could not put everyone at risk. Especially little Elena Rose. Her little niece was only two weeks old. Why she'd soon be three weeks old.

Family? That was what she had here. Gil thought it should be enough. She wished it could be. She knew he was right. The past had too great a hold on her, but she didn't know any other way to ease that hold than confront Frank's stepbrother. Why had he never told her the man's name? Why hadn't she thought to ask?

A rustling to her right sent her heart into a frenzied patter. What was wrong with her that she hadn't even thought to get her club to defend herself and Anna?

She pushed to her feet and edged toward the wagon intending to belatedly arm herself.

Then Gil stepped from the shadows. He saw her. Read the fear in her face. "It's just me." He crossed to her side, took Anna in one arm and pulled Judith close with the other.

Judith struggled to fill her lungs past the tightness in her chest.

Gil rubbed her arm. "I saw no one out there. I heard the men still searching for the oxen and mules but they will soon have to abandon the task. With the cloud cover that's moved in there won't even be enough moonlight to see the ground before them."

Judith's lungs finally decided to work and she relaxed into Gil's chest. He was right about the darkness. It felt heavy and threatening. "Did you find a place for the night?" she whispered.

"I did. Here's what we're going to do. We'll put Anna to sleep in the wagon. You'll join her. I'll leave you for a bit until it would appear you have gone to sleep. During that time I will set out my bedroll so anyone listening will think I am about to bed down. You gather up what bedding you can carry. I'll carry my bedroll and we'll slip away."

"May God keep us safe."

"Amen. Let's sit down. Try and appear normal."

"It's hard when I think those men might be

lingering nearby, perhaps even close enough to hear us."

"Let's make sure they hear the right things. Why don't you recite some of the verses you know?"

She chuckled to think evil men might be forced to listen to God's Word and she recited the Twenty-third Psalm. By the time she finished, her fear had subsided. God would lead them and protect them. The One Hundred and Third Psalm was also reassuring and she quoted it from beginning to end.

They sat side by side, his arm about her and he tightened his grasp. "I like the thought that God forgives us, heals our diseases and redeems us from destruction."

"Me, too."

"Anna's asleep."

"I'll put her to bed. I might as well go myself. It's too dark to do anything else and morning comes early." If anyone listened, they would hear ordinary night time talk.

Gil carried Anna to the back of the wagon and handed her up to Judith.

"Goodnight," he said, squeezing her hand.

"Goodnight," she answered. She settled Anna, wrapping her in a blanket. The other bedding she rolled together so it would be easy to carry. She found her club and put it with her bundle then sat to wait for Gil's signal.

She listened to him moving quietly, but making enough noise that anyone who might be waiting for him to go to sleep would think he had stretched out under the wagon. The minutes ticked by. She strained to hear any sound. The nearby camp had fallen silent. Anna breathed heavily. A coyote called and was answered by a dozen others. Her nerves jangled.

The mules brayed and she jerked to her feet, putting herself between the back gate and Anna. No intruders would get to the baby without confronting Judith. She had tied the front so tightly that she'd hear anyone attempting to enter that way. But if men came from both ends, how could she protect Anna? She moved closer to the baby intending to cover her with her body if necessary.

"Judith?" The whisper came from the back gate.

"Gil?"

"Are you ready? Hand me Anna."

She lifted the well-wrapped baby to Gil, grabbed her bundle of bedding, took a good hold on her club and managed to silently climb down.

Gil had his arms full with Anna and his own bedding, but she clung to his elbow as he led her into the trees. He moved slowly, silently. She did her best to move silently as well but she lacked his expertise and there was an unmistakable sound of dry leaves brushing against her.

He stopped and pulled her forward. "Duck your head," he whispered in her ear.

She did so and could barely make out a tiny hollow in the bushes.

He pushed in behind her. "Sit," he whispered and

she did so. "We'll spend the night here." His warm breath brushed her cheeks. "Get comfortable."

The space was small allowing her to move her bundle only a few inches at a time but she managed to spread her blankets and lay on top of them, then pull them over her. As soon as she was done, Gil did the same. They lay side by side, crowded together in the tiny hollow, Anna pressed safely between them. Judith wrapped an arm about the baby. Gil covered them both with an arm.

Their heads almost touched and she whispered, "What were the mules fussing about?"

"They thought the coyotes were too close, but the noise came at the right time for us to escape."

The air was cool and damp and the cold from the ground made its way through her covers but she wasn't overly uncomfortable. In fact, it was almost cozy with Gil beside her, his arm warm and heavy around her.

She didn't expect to sleep but must have drifted off because the next thing she knew Gil touched her cheek.

"Wake up. It's time to go back to the wagon." He waited until she was alert then slipped from his bed and rolled the blankets together. She did the same. He took Anna and they slipped toward their isolated camp. Dawn lightened the horizon.

Anna wakened as they reached the wagon and let out a wail. Her voice was hoarse and she sounded irritable.

"Take her." Gil sounded concerned. He built a fire, with no apparent concern for being discovered.

Judith moved toward the warmth of the blaze. Anna fussed. She did not like having her sleep disturbed.

"Let me have a look at her."

Judith wondered at the anxious way Gil spoke. He caught Anna's chin and dipped his head to see her better. "Her nose is running." He touched her forehead and slowly straightened to look sorrowfully into Judith's eyes.

Judith blinked before the despair she saw in his gaze and then looked carefully at Anna.

She touched the baby's forehead. It didn't seem overly warm, but she had a runny nose and a hoarse throat. It couldn't be. It simply could not be.

11

Gil held Judith and Anna a moment longer than went to tend the mules. Men from the main camp left in search of the missing stock. Without them the wagon train would not move. He watched them depart. He had never felt so helpless. He couldn't join them in searching for the animals even though the isolation period was over because now Anna had a runny nose and they must start all over again.

He pushed his fist to his stomach, as if the action could undo the knot in there. Of course, it wasn't being forced to stand by while others worked that bothered him. It was the helplessness he felt in face of Anna's condition. He couldn't do anything to prevent illness, to protect those he cared about, and to eventually make the home he wanted.

Buck rode toward Gil. Gil held up his hand to signal him to stop.

"You can rejoin us now," Buck called.

"Anna has a runny nose."

Buck sat back in his saddle. "Did she catch a chill?"

Air wheezed from Gil's lungs. A chill. He'd never thought of the possibility. "How do we tell the difference?"

"We have no choice but to wait and see. Watch for swollen glands and drooling and then …" He didn't finish. Gil knew someone with diphtheria stood a chance of being unable to breathe because of the membrane that grew over their throat.

"Soon enough you'll know if it's more than a cold."

Gil nodded. Even Buck couldn't bring himself to say the word aloud any more than Gil could. He silently thanked the man for that inability.

The women had gathered at the side of their wagons, watching and waiting. No doubt expecting Judith to rejoin them.

Buck rode toward them.

Gil watched their faces cloud with worry as Buck relayed the news. Having done so Buck rode on to help bring back the missing stock.

Judith joined him, Anna in her arms and stared across at her friends.

"We'll be praying," Donna Grace called.

"Please do," Judith called back.

Gil put his arm about her and they watched the women return to their cook fires. Only then did they go to their own fire and sit down for breakfast.

Anna didn't want to eat. She wanted to be held and

Gil was only too happy to oblige. He ate his food with little enthusiasm and failed to find enjoyment in his coffee. He guessed Judith had a similar problem for she pushed her food around on her plate and seemed to have forgotten to drink from her cup.

The baby fell asleep in his arms. Every few minutes he checked her for any sign of fever. "She doesn't feel warm." He wondered if Judith had heard the symptoms Buck had mentioned or if she knew them without hearing them spoken but he wasn't going to ask and give her any more reason to watch Anna as keenly as he was.

His stomach muscles clenched again just as they had earlier. How would he endure watching Anna grow more ill and—

He choked off the thoughts and finished his now-cold breakfast and downed his equally cold coffee.

Judith took care of the dishes. "How long will we be here?"

He understood she meant the delay and welcomed a reminder to think of something other than Anna's illness. "Until the draft animals are found."

"I might as well put the delay to good use." She scurried about setting to stew the buffalo meat Buck had left for them.

Mary Mae called from the other wagons. "We're going to the water to do some laundry."

Judith watched them depart then turned away. "I suppose I shouldn't think of washing anything until…"

Until they knew if Anna had a chill or diphtheria.

They both looked at the baby. Gil had laid her on a bed of blankets close to the fire where she would be warm. Neither of them seemed inclined to go more than a few steps away from her.

Not that there was anything they could do to prevent the progression of the disease except pray. His silent prayer formed a litany in his brain. *Please spare her, God. Please spare her.*

Gil wished he could ride out and help with the livestock. He wished he could go fishing. Not that he could see himself able to leave Anna's side, but waiting was the hardest thing he'd ever had to do.

The women returned with wet items that they draped over ropes strung from wagon to wagon. They paused to ask after Anna.

Gil and Judith had nothing to report. Anna had wakened once, fussed a little. Judith had given her a drink, and wiped her nose and then she'd gone back to sleep.

"She's able to swallow," Judith had whispered.

Gil had nodded, relieved. At least she wasn't strangling.

The women returned to their chores. Judith came to his side and took his hand. "I wish to hear you pray." Her eyes were wide, searching, wanting. "It encourages me."

He took her hands. "Then by all means." He closed his eyes and stood toe to toe with Judith. "God our Father, we are concerned for our little child. We don't want to lose her nor do we want to have her suffer.

Please, may whatever is making her like this be nothing more than a cold. Please, Father."

Judith squeezed his hands hard. "Please, God. We ask for her life. We ask that we might have the joy of seeing her grow into adulthood."

Neither of them said Amen. He was the first to move and he simply pulled their joined hands to his chest and pressed his forehead to hers. He had found something with Judith and Anna that he had long sought after though he hadn't known it was what he sought until now. If he lost Anna…. If Judith insisted on pursuing the man with no name….

Closing his eyes, he held her tightly. How long before they knew Anna's future?

Lowing of oxen and braying of mules informed them the animals had been found. Their own mules brayed a response which wakened Anna and she cried, her voice hoarse.

Judith offered her a drink. She took a little then fussed and pushed the cup away.

Judith handed her a biscuit. Anna took one bite then wailed.

Gil went to the baby and picked her up. She stuck two fingers in her mouth and then pulled them out, hung her head and cried.

"Poor baby," he crooned. "You're miserable and don't understand why. I wish you could tell us what's wrong."

Judith pressed to his shoulder and stroked Anna's head. "If only we knew."

"We have to wait and see." He tried to sound comforting but wondered how well he succeeded. Judith brushed the back of her hand over Anna's cheeks.

"At least she hasn't gotten worse. That's good news, isn't it?"

"I want to hope so." He knew it sometimes took days for the disease to reach its peak. He had never seen anyone strangled by the membrane that grew in the back of the throat but, like most people, had heard the horrible tales.

The animals were brought to the circled wagons.

Gil expected they would now depart but instead, the men milled about. He handed Anna to Judith and stepped away, hoping someone would inform him what was going on.

Buck and several of the teamsters conferred. Gil could not see Luke or Warren which seemed a little odd. Then Buck rode toward Gil stopping at a distance. "We're still missing too many animals to continue. Luke, Warren and some of the others are still looking for them. I'm going to ride out and see if I can help. Keep your rifle handy."

Gil nodded. He too wondered if this was a trap by the raiders. Draw as many men away from the wagons as they could and then attack the wagons.

Judith joined him. "Are my brothers in danger?"

Gil couldn't deny they might be. "They're seasoned travellers and know to be cautious. I can't imagine them riding into danger. Besides, there's half a dozen men with them."

Anna fussed and Judith bounced her up and down, trying to calm her. "Can you find the sugar rag? I'll see if she'll take it."

Glad to have something useful to do, he climbed into the wagon and located the rag. He dampened it then gave it to Anna. She sucked a moment then let out a wail.

Mrs. Shepton called to them. "Are you sure she isn't teething?"

Judith and Gil looked at each other. He read her answer which was the same as his. How would they know?

Mrs. Shepton took a step closer and might have continued on but Mary Mae caught her arm. They had a short conversation which ended when Mrs. Shepton nodded.

Judith grinned at Gil. "I'm guessing Mary Mae told the preacher's wife that she couldn't cross over to here even on a noble deed."

He chuckled at her wording.

Mrs. Shepton called again. "Look inside her mouth. See if a tooth is poking through or if her gums are swollen."

Judith took the sugar rag from Anna and she promptly opened her mouth to wail. Judith peered into her mouth. "Her gums are red and swollen," she told Mrs. Shepton.

"Trying rubbing them and see if that helps."

Judith did so and Anna stopped crying. "It worked."

Mrs. Shepton clapped. "It could be all that's wrong. We're all praying. God bless you all."

"Thanks." Gil and Judith called in unison.

They smiled at each other, Judith's eyes brighter than Gil had seen them in several hours.

"Teething," she said. "I hope that's all it is." She continued to massage Anna's gums.

"We'll have to watch and wait to be sure." He kissed Anna then, before he could talk himself into being more cautious, he kissed Judith's forehead.

She lifted her head and gave him a smile that melted every resistance he'd ever dreamed of and he caught her lips in a kiss as sweet as fresh honey and as gentle as morning dew. He withdrew. Saw the surprised look on her face and perhaps something more—a pleased, contented look.

"I'm going to get some wood chopped while we're here." Feeling considerably lighter than he had for a long time, he took his axe in one hand, his rifle in the other and went into the woods to find fuel.

He had gathered a decent bit of wood, had gone back for more when the sound of gunshots reached him. He straightened, lifted his rifle and listened. Several more gunshots rang out and then the thunder of many hooves. Forgetting everything but Judith and Anna, he raced through the trees, unmindful of the slapping branches and thorny bushes that tore at him.

Judith stood, wide eyed and holding Anna, when he reached their campsite. "What's going on?" she asked.

"We'll soon enough know. Take Anna and stay in the wagon until it's safe to come out." He called for the others to take shelter, but they already had. The men with them had positioned themselves to protect the wagons.

Not wanting to draw fire toward the wagon, Gil flattened himself on the ground close to the trees, set his rifle ready and tensed as the hoof beats drew closer.

"Hi Yiii."

He recognized Warren's call but wasn't about to let his guard down. The missing animals panted to a halt. Men he recognized as drovers and freighters drove the animals.

Gil waited a full minute to see if anyone else rode toward them. Seeing no one, he got to his feet.

Judith poked her head out. "Is it safe?"

Buck rode up. "We've seen the last of that bunch of men." He offered no more explanation and Gil asked for none.

"It's safe," he told Judith and she jumped down with Anna in her arms.

The baby continued to fuss but he worried less, prepared to believe it was nothing more than sore gums.

Buck had gone to speak to the men and inspect the animals. He returned to calling distance. "We'll spend another night here while the animals rest. Some have their tongues hanging out."

"Anything I can do to help?" Gil asked.

"Stay away from others until we know it's not diphtheria. That's the best you can do for all of us."

Gil knew it to be true but being idle did not sit well with him.

WITH NO NEED TO hurry and be on the trail they ate a leisurely noon meal. Judith knew Gil was restless, but gratitude flowed through her veins. The raiders had been driven off. She didn't ask, didn't want to know how many had died. She had every reason to think Anna was only teething and as if to prove it, the baby pulled Judith's fingers to her mouth and gnawed on them. Unfortunately, she had her incisors and Judith had to be careful not to get bitten.

Despite Gil's longing look toward the other men who scurried about taking care of the tired animals and gathering wood for their wagons, Judith appreciated having him nearby. His presence made her feel safe and liked.

Liked? She shook her head at such silliness. But the idea lingered. He went to get more wood to store in the rack under the wagon. The sound of him tramping through the trees, the sound of an axe cutting wood, the scent of beans baking and meat stewing, a baby holding to her hand so she could bite down on her finger—they were all satisfying. As if she'd been born for this. A wife and a mother. If she admitted it, she'd have to say it was what she'd always wanted. She'd hoped for it with Frank. How many times had she, in her mind, decorated the rooms of the house he said was his?

It never was his but she didn't know that until later. She'd imagined children playing and doing lessons. She'd seen herself sewing little garments and Frank sitting nearby reading as the children slept.

It was not to be. But now she was a wife and a mother. Perhaps her dreams had simply found their fulfillment elsewhere.

But what about Frank's stepbrother? Her contentment fled, replaced by a hard knot of sorrow, guilt and a hefty dose of blame.

Gil returned with an armload of firewood, whistling as he put it under the wagon and she forgot about her goal as she rejoiced. "I won't have to burn buffalo chips for a few days."

He sat back and grinned at her. "I hope you don't mind."

His teasing tickled her insides and she laughed. "I am grateful. In fact, I am going to make a special dessert for you tonight. What's your favorite?"

"Apple pie." His eyes darkened and seemed to see something in the distance. Then he brought his gaze to her, soft and so full of caring that her throat closed off.

Was this what she wanted? A man who cared for her, protected her—but did she deserve it?

Where had that come from?

He watched her. "You look like someone stepped on your grave. What's wrong?"

She wanted to tell him. Didn't want to tell him. It was foolish. Made her sound like she felt sorry for herself.

He closed the distance between them, set Anna on the ground, ignored her whining and grasped Judith by her shoulders. "Something's wrong. Tell me what it is."

She rocked her head back and forth, but he caught her chin and stopped it. She tried to look beyond him but something about his quiet insistence drew her gaze to his warm, steady, demanding, caring eyes. Try as she wanted, she could not hold back her thoughts.

"I don't deserve to have you care about me." Why couldn't she say that without sounding as whiny as Anna?

He stared at her then pulled her to his chest and rubbed her back. "Is that how Frank's death makes you feel? That you don't deserve affection?"

"I didn't know that's how I felt." With her face pressed to the warmth of his shirt she found she could speak calmly. She twisted her fingers into the fabric.

"It isn't true. You must know that."

"In my head I do. But in my thoughts, I can't help but think a person gets what they deserve in life."

"Do you really think that?" His soft voice held no condemnation, only gentle doubt.

"I don't know. Maybe."

"By that reasoning, then I deserve what Lillian did to me and Anna deserves to lose her parents."

She jerked back and stared into his face. "I would never suggest anything like that."

"You're saying it isn't true then?"

"It wasn't your fault and Anna is a baby. She's done nothing wrong." She picked up the fussing baby and cradled her against her neck. Anna sobbed softly as if wanting Judith to make her feel better.

"You did nothing wrong either. You aren't to blame for what happened any more than Anna is. It doesn't mean you don't deserve good things." He caught her chin in the palm of his hand and drew her gaze to his. "You are worthy of being loved and cherished."

He held her gaze, his open and…she tried to think what it was she saw. Tried just as hard not to admit it. She saw the very things she wanted—acceptance and value. Dare she believe it? Or was she seeing more than he offered?

Anna continued to sob quietly. Judith tore her gaze from Gil's. She wasn't ready to throw caution to the wind. "I'll see if she wants something to eat."

She spent the next hour taking care of Anna and amusing her while Gil greased the wheels and checked over the harnessing. Judith glanced toward the other wagons and saw the men doing the same…using the time to make sure everything was in top shape for the journey they would continue tomorrow.

Awkwardness made her movements jerky as she served supper. Why had she spoken her thoughts aloud? His answer had upset her careful plans. She felt torn between wanting what Gil offered—at least what she thought he offered—and the need to confront Frank's stepbrother.

She simply could not choose between the two because, despite what Gil said, she felt she was somehow to blame for Frank's death and the only way to make it right was to find his stepbrother. She had to keep reminding herself because it would be far too easy to shove it aside and take up a new life with Gil which she fully meant to do…but not until she'd eased her burden of guilt and failure by making the other Jones man admit his share of responsibility in Frank's death.

Gil sat across the fire from her, studying her. He slid closer to hold her hands as he said grace. She would have refused him except then he would guess how upset she was. The last thing she needed would be for him to try to make her agree with his point of view. So she allowed him to hold her hand as he prayed. She tried not to hear his words as he asked for safety and for her peace of mind. Wasn't he supposed to be thanking God for the food? At his amen, she quickly pulled back, grateful that Anna wanted to be fed off Judith's plate. It gave her a fine excuse to ignore Gil. Not that she was unaware of his watchful gaze. Let him think what he wanted. She didn't expect him to understand what she must do.

A niggling little thought plagued her.

Did *she* understand why she thought she must do

this? When she left Independence it had been so clear, her reasons so simple. Nothing had changed.

Except she'd entered into a marriage and acquired a little girl as daughter. Indeed, her whole world had shifted on its axis.

But did that change what she'd set out to do?

GIL WATCHED the expressions on Judith's face shift through a range of emotions—upset, confusion, stubbornness and back to confusion. He wished he could read her thoughts. Wished even more that he could make her understand that she wasn't to blame for Frank's death and finding the stepbrother would not in any way change what had happened. But he'd tried and failed to make her see that. That failure weighed upon his shoulders. He wanted a wife, a family and a home. Perhaps he didn't deserve them.

He chuckled.

Judith stared at him. "What's so funny?"

"You. Me. Our situation." The more he thought about it, the more he laughed.

Her scowl sobered him. "I don't find it the least bit amusing."

"I was sitting here thinking about what I want. And then I thought, maybe I don't deserve it. Isn't that funny? I just finished explaining to you how you deserve good things then I tell myself the same thing you told yourself." He knew he sounded confused but he wasn't in the least.

"Still don't think it's funny." She continued to study him, her eyes so hungry that he forgot everything but his desire to fill that need.

"Judith, don't we deserve whatever happiness our marriage and little Anna can provide?" He heard the pleading in his voice, but didn't care whether she heard it.

She shifted her gaze past him then brought it back.

He knew by the brittleness in her eyes that she wasn't about to agree.

"I am thinking of our happiness. That's why I must do what I've set out to do."

"I don't understand. Maybe I never will."

She turned away and the knot in his stomach returned. He knew rubbing it would not ease it.

Only one thing would and Judith wasn't about to give him that. She had promised to be faithful to him. Not that Judith was unfaithful in the same way as Lillian. But she chose finding a nameless man in a vast uncharted territory to making a home with him.

If only he could find a way to make her leave the past and face a future with him and Anna—a future free of old sorrows.

He amused Anna while Judith did the few dishes and cleaned up the camp area then she prepared the baby for bed.

"I'm going to see if she will sleep." With a quick goodnight, Judith climbed into the wagon.

Gil knew she had retired early to get away from him. He tossed the dregs of his cup on the flickering flames. What could he do to make her choose him over the nameless man she sought?

He left the warmth of the fire, driven by unanswered questions and longing that came from deep inside. He strode toward the trees then turned and strode back. One thought grew clear—he wanted a wife who was faithful to him. With hurried steps he made another circuit to the trees and back.

They barely knew each other when they'd been thrown into this marriage. There'd been none of the customary time of getting to know each other and discover traits they admired.

Another circuit brought him back to the fire and in the light from the flames, he saw the truth with clarity.

He must court her as she deserved to be courted and she would learn to care about him above all else. Except her faith, of course. That went without saying. But above her search for a nameless man. All he wanted was for her to put her past behind her and embrace a future with him.

The warmth of the fire filled his heart. He had a plan. One, he was certain, destined to bring Judith's heart and loyalty to him.

12

Judith wakened to the sounds of oxen lowing, mules braying and harnesses rattling. Dawn was a promise in the eastern sky.

Anna woke and crawled to Judith to babble about the morning.

Judith sat up. "You're better?" No more hoarse voice. No more runny nose. "Let me see in your mouth." She opened wide to show Anna what she meant and Anna imitated her. It was too dark to see if the tooth had emerged but Judith reached in and felt the hard little nub. "Thank you, God." She wanted to sing the words.

In seconds she pulled her dress on and left the wagon, Anna in her arms.

Gil and the mules were missing. She breathed back her disappointment at having to wait for him to bring them back from water before she could share her news. At the circle of wagons, fires burned, women tended food and men brought in animals. Everyone was in a hurry to leave this place.

None more than Judith. There'd been too much danger and fear here. She couldn't wait to move on.

"Here." She gave Anna a biscuit to gnaw on while she turned her attention to preparing breakfast.

Coffee waited when Gil returned and she handed him a cup. "Good news," she said. "Anna is feeling better."

He swallowed some coffee then squatted in front of Anna. She reached out for him to pick her up. Chuckling, he lifted her and stood, taking in her happy smile.

"Her tooth is through," Judith said.

Gil whooped, startling Anna who buried her face into his chest. His yell brought the attention of those in the other camp. "She's better," he called.

The others clapped.

Buck rode close. "Tell me what's going on."

"She has a new tooth," Gil said. "And no more runny nose or any sign of being sick. It was just the tooth bothering her."

Buck studied them a moment. "If she's still fine by noon, I'll let you rejoin the others."

"Thanks."

Judith had joined Gil and he pulled her to his side. She fought and lost a brief struggle with herself to resist his affections. The way he treated her made it harder and harder to remember why she had set out on this journey.

He looked down at her. "You'll be happy to be with your friends again."

She grasped at the diversion. "It will be nice. And you'll be glad to be back at your scouting."

"I might have mixed feelings about that."

She had every intention of slipping from his embrace, but his words stalled her and she looked into his steady gaze. Did she read a promise there?

He didn't give her a chance to ask what he meant as he tipped his forehead to hers and said, "I've enjoyed being just the three of us." His words, uttered in a low, deep voice settled into her heart with the intent of setting up residence there.

Somehow she managed to make herself return to the fire and announce breakfast was ready.

"I'll pray." He sat beside her and reach for her hand.

"Lord God, healer and defender, we thank You for Anna's well-being and for rescue from the raiders and for the safe return of the animals." His voice deepened. "I thank You for the food You have provided but even more, I thank You for a wife and child. Amen."

He had never before spoken of gratitude for a wife. Why now? It wasn't as if she'd fallen in with his plans for the future. In fact, she continued to resist his wish that she forget about her past. Judith hurriedly turned her attention to serving the food. She tried to avoid Gil's gaze, but when Anna said, "Umm, umm," and leaned forward begging for food, she laughed and could not resist sharing the enjoyment of this child with Gil.

They were too busy the next little while for her to concern herself with how things might look in the future. They ate a hurried breakfast, cleaned up their campsite and prepared for the day's journey.

Gil helped her to the wagon seat and handed Anna up. The baby found her collection of rocks and greeted them like long lost friends.

Judith laughed.

"Good to see you so happy," Gil said.

Judith looked toward the other wagons, pulling into a long line. "By noon we'll be with the others."

She expected they would be on their way but she'd forgotten they had to cross Cow Creek. They pulled up to the side of the other wagons. The stream looked lower than the Little Arkansas. She mentioned it to Gil.

"Don't let it fool you. The bottom is muddy and the wheels sink to their axles. It's a difficult crossing. It will take time."

The lighter wagons went first then one by one, the heavier ones, each struggling through the deceptively placid creek. She wondered aloud at their hurry this morning. "I could have washed every item of bedding and clothing while we waited."

Gil alternately stood by the wagon and paced back and forth. He heard her comment. "I wish I could be helping."

There was nothing she could say to make it so for

him. By noon, they'd be able to join the others. But until then they must wait.

The crossing was soon complete and they continued on their way. Despite the jostling and bouncing and hard seat of the wagon it was good to be back on the trail but it made it far too easy to do nothing but think. Judith tried to keep her mind on her reason for her journey. But the future beckoned. A future shared with Gil and Anna. In an attempt to divert herself from the confusion of her thoughts, she turned to Gil.

"You've told me little about Lillian. What was she like?"

"I would think what I've told you is enough for you to draw your own conclusions." His voice had grown hard. Such a contrast to how he spoke to Judith and Anna.

"How did you meet her?"

"Why do you ask? That's in the past and I don't care to go back."

"Maybe—" She spoke slowly, forming her thoughts as she continued, "if I can understand how you are able to forget the past I might learn how to do it." She felt his study of her, but kept her attention on the mules. She wasn't sure she wanted to forget—not until she'd dealt with it the only way she knew how. Then perhaps, it could be set aside. But until then it simply wasn't acceptable to not do what she could to make things right. For Frank's sake as well as her own.

Gil accepted her answer. "Perhaps it will. I met her

in my father's store. She was—or rather, seemed—so sweet and innocent. She wanted to know if we had a certain color thread. She kept her eyes lowered, stealing only a quick glance at me as if too shy to actually meet my look. I thought she was the perfect woman. I learned she had recently come to live with her aunt and I arranged for a proper introduction."

Judith tried in vain to make this picture of a sweet young lady fit the one she had from Gil's few comments. "So you courted her?"

"I did. We went to church together and church socials and literary evenings. We visited in each other's home, always with my father or her aunt to chaperone."

Judith tried not to grin at the difference in how she and Gil had met and married.

"Did you never suspect she wasn't all you thought?"

He didn't answer immediately and she turned just enough to be able to see his face and take in the hard set of his jaw. He lifted one shoulder. "I had noticed her flirting with men a time or two but put it down to her innocence. I told myself she didn't know how it appeared to the man and I spoke to her about it. She was immediately contrite. Turns out she was neither shy nor contrite. I had been duped from the beginning."

She wrapped her fingers around his hand. "I'm sorry. I know how much it must have hurt."

"It's in the past. I only care about the present and the future."

A small sigh escaped. "So you've said." She didn't understand how it was possible.

"There is no value in letting the past weigh one down."

"Sometimes the past needs justice."

They fell silent, each clinging to their opinion. Judith did not like being at odds with Gil, but he was so stubborn. "Doesn't the Bible say, 'No man, having put his hand to the plow and looking back, is fit for the Kingdom of God.'?"

"I don't think it means something like what you have in mind."

She would not acknowledge that he was right and felt childish for not doing so. "I must do what I must do."

He reached for her hand and held it gently. "Judith, I am tired of having this same argument over and over. Nothing ever changes. I'd much rather enjoy your company and little Anna's without this constant disagreement. I'm satisfied that we'll reach some sort of compromise when the time comes. Can we agree to let it rest until we reach our destination?"

She knew he hoped she'd change her mind before they reached Santa Fe. A great portion of her wished she could. But he was right. There was nothing to be gained by going over the same ground again and again. She wouldn't mind forgetting it for the time being. "Agreed." She turned her palm to his and they intertwined their fingers.

"That's better." He grinned at her in a way that almost made her forget everything else.

They rode on in companionable quiet for a time.

Suddenly she thought of something. "Where did your stepbrother go?"

"I don't know. I haven't personally heard from him or seen him since he left. I know he contacted my pa and his ma from time to time for more money and always had a different address but when I tried to find him at the various places he wasn't there and no one seemed to recall him. I can only assume he used a temporary address purposely so he couldn't be found."

"You think he was misusing the funds?"

"He always borrowed. Never returned." He shook her hand gently. "I have a feeling this discussion is leading back to the same one we have decided to leave behind."

She nodded. "I suppose I was hoping to make you understand my feelings seeing as you have a similar stepbrother."

"I thought you were going to make me an apple pie."

It took a moment for her to realize what he meant. "I must have forgotten."

"I haven't."

She knew he teased and she laughed. "I'll have to see what I can do tonight."

"If we rejoin the others I suppose that means I'll have to share the pie with them."

She loved the way his voice filled with sorrow even

if he only pretended it mattered that much. "Seems only right." Her gaze went to the wagons traveling to their right.

A short time later, Buck called for a nooning halt. He rode toward them. "How's the little one?"

Gil pulled Anna to his knee. "Wave at the man."

She did so.

"She's fine. We're all fine."

"Welcome back." He waved them toward the others and Gil drove the wagon over to fall in behind Luke's wagon.

Judith jumped down as soon as it was safe and was engulfed in hugs from Donna Grace and Mary Mae. Then her brothers shook Gil's hand and patted her shoulders, welcoming them back.

Reverend and Mrs. Shepton also extended their welcome. Polly and her father joined in the greetings and the teamsters waved and cheered.

Buck sat astride his horse, smiling. "We ain't got all day," he said after he'd let them say their hellos.

Judith joined the others in serving a cold meal that they ate hurriedly. It felt so good to be with others that she met Gil's eyes and smiled, letting him know how happy she was.

To her surprise, he didn't smile back and her pleasure waned. She knew he was glad that none of them had come down with that dreadful disease so why didn't he share her pleasure? Had he been serious when he said he would miss having her and Anna as his sole companions? She couldn't pull from his gaze and felt something warm and sweet pool in her stomach.

"While the men rest we have time to rearrange a few things," Donna Grace said.

Judith hurried to the back of the wagon Donna Grace and Luke shared with baby Elena Rose. "Wow. It's really crowded in here." Much of the stuff belonged to Judith. "Thank you for not throwing it out."

Donna Grace chuckled. "Luke threatened to when we almost mired down crossing Cow Creek but I persuaded him not to."

Judith laughed at the idea of her brother acquiescing to Donna Grace's wishes.

They moved Judith's trunk and other belongings to the other wagon before it was time to move on.

They were ready to leave when she realized how very different things were going to be.

Gil had left a few minutes ago with Buck and returned on horseback. He paused at her side. "I'll be scouting again. Warren will drive the wagon." He touched the brim of his hat that shaded his eyes. She couldn't be sure that she saw regret they would no longer travel together or if the feeling came from her own thoughts.

"OF COURSE," she murmured. This was what they'd expected to happen but as he rode away, she couldn't believe how much she missed him already.

GIL LOVED the solitude of guiding. He could ride for hours and never speak to anyone except maybe his faithful old horse, Slack, who had heard most of his concerns and doubts over the years.

"You've been a faithful friend," he told the horse. "But I gotta say you aren't much of a conversationalist. 'Course you don't ask any questions either. Guess I should be grateful for that."

Judith's questions about Ollie had renewed thoughts of the past. "I thought I had them over and done with. Seems I'm forever letting myself care about those who don't necessarily return the feeling." There was Pa who put Ollie first. There was Ollie whom Gil had wanted more than anything to be special friends with. Instead, Ollie had left their parents destitute and never contacted Gil again. There was Lillian who had shown him in the worst way just how little she cared about his feelings.

"And now there's Judith."

Slack twitched his ears.

"You don't know what I'm talking about but here's the thing. She's promised to be faithful, but she's put me in an awkward position. Seems if I don't go along with her in looking for this Jones person, she will go on her own. I can't allow that." He sighed. "Yup. That's the way it is. I'll have to tag along after her on some wild goose chase that might last until we're both old and gray." He didn't know when he'd made the decision to go with her, but perhaps he'd known all along it was what he must do.

"Unless she changes her mind before then and decides to leave the past and ride into the future with me." It was his greatest hope.

"Maybe I can do things to make her see that's what she wants." He came full circle back to the courting idea. Although he kept his ears and eyes opened and made sure no more raiders nor other dangers lurked about to put the wagon train in danger, he also planned how he could court Judith under their circumstances.

A movement in the distance caught his attention and he reined toward a dip in the land and watched the speck. It didn't move. He couldn't make out if it was a man on horseback or an animal. One way to find out. Keeping Slack to a slow pace he made his way around the curve of the dip, pausing often to see if the object remained. He thought he saw it move once but it might have been only the wavy lines rising from the warm earth.

In a few more minutes he rose from the hollow and stood in plain view, waiting for the thing to move. He leaned over Slack's neck.

"Guess we'll have to take our chances, old boy." He rode forward and suddenly reined in. What he saw was not a man but something made to look like one, stuffed pants and shirt tied to the back of a horse.

He'd almost ridden straight into a trap. He glanced about. A rider approached from his left, another from his right. The pretend man was replaced by a real one who rode toward him.

Gil reined about and galloped back into the hollow and made for a line of trees along a little draw that would lead back to Cow Creek.

His direction took him away from the wagon train though the dust from it could be seen by anyone who cared to have a look. It caused him to wonder why these men were after him. Apart from the fact he was alone.

In the past, he had thought only of saving his own hide. Now he thought only of Judith and Anna and his desire to share a home with them. His mind raced as he sought for a plan.

Slack galloped into the bushes of the draw.

A shot rang out and dirt puffed up to his right. A sharpshooter with a good rifle who could end Gil's life here and now.

Gil lay over Slack's neck. "Think you can outrun them?" he asked the horse who already panted.

He didn't take time to offer a formal prayer, but he threw his wordless prayer to heaven. He had been in danger hundreds of times but now it mattered that he live. Others mattered to him more than his own life.

A dark spot ahead caught his attention. A hollow in the dirt bank. He reined in without further consideration and guided Slack into the spot that was barely big enough for his horse and himself. "Good boy," he told his cooperative mount.

The sound of galloping horses reached him. They

would soon catch up. He readied himself, his rifle aimed at the place where they would appear.

The leader thundered into sight. Gil fired and the man's gun flew into the air. The horse reared. The man lost his seat and landed on the ground. He scurried into bushes that did little to hide him and nothing to protect him.

The second man pulled back but not before he was in Gil's sights. He shot at Gil and Gil returned fire. The man rolled from his saddle to the ground, injured or worse.

The third man rode away and Gil fired after him more as a warning than anything. He emerged from his little cave, his gun trained on the man cowering in the bushes. "Come out."

The man emerged, his hands above his head. Gil nudged the other man with his boot. He'd be a danger to no one ever again.

But what was he to do with the man before him? He studied him. Didn't recognize him. Why did he wonder if it was Ollie? Judith had gotten him to thinking of his stepbrother. What if he was the stepbrother Judith sought. "What's your name?"

"Who wants to know?"

Gil had no intention of shooting the man but he didn't need to know that. "Might be nice to put something on the cross that marks your grave."

"Just put Captain on the cross."

Gil had to give the man credit for not showing any fear. "Why were you after me?"

The man laughed. "I thought you were someone else. Me and some others were supposed to meet and share our goods, if you know what I mean."

Gil did. Good stolen from others. He wondered if they were associates of those who meant to rob the wagon train. "Might be those others met an untimely end."

The man gave him a hard stare. "Let's get this over with."

Gil considered his options. He had two horses, a man with a bad attitude, a dead man who—no matter what he'd done—deserved a decent burial and a third man who might even now be drawing a bead on him. Sweat broke out on Gil's brow but he would not give an inch.

"You got a shovel?"

"What business is that of yours?"

Gil signaled the man toward his horse, saw shovel hanging from the saddle bags. "Start digging."

"Says who?"

"Dig or I'll leave two bodies out here for the wolves to enjoy."

The man cursed him soundly then set to digging. Gil backed into the protection of the cave and kept his rifle trained on the man and tried to think what to do.

At the sound of an approaching horse, he stood to attention. "If this is your friend, you better hope he doesn't come in shooting because you'll be the first to die."

"Curses to you." The man raised the shovel as if he planned to attack Gil with it.

Gil hoped he wouldn't be forced to shoot another man.

A voice called from the ridge above them. "I wouldn't do that if I were you."

Gil knew that voice and grinned. "You been following me around, Buck?"

"Nope, but when I heard gunshots I decided to investigate." He rode down, leading the third man bound and tied to his horse.

"What do you plan to do with this pair?" Gil asked.

"Haven't decided. Sure don't want to babysit them. But I thought I might turn them over to Frenchie. He enjoys having men like this to play with."

Buck referred to one of the teamsters.

"Yeah, Frenchie loves picking up grown men, holding them over his head then slamming them into the ground. He'll like having some new playthings." Gil grinned at Buck as the color drained from the faces of their prisoners. Gil knew, as did Buck, that although Frenchie was big, he didn't have a violent nature. But for the safety of those in the wagon train, it might be best not to inform their prisoners of that fact. A little fear would keep them on their best behavior.

They allowed Captain to finish digging the grave.

"What name shall I put on the marker?" Gil asked. He'd found a thick branch that would have to do.

"Blade will do."

Gil didn't ask why that name. He carved the letters

into the wood, took the shovel that he'd made Captain relinquish and drove the stake into the ground.

He tied Captain, secured him to his horse and they made their way to the wagon train where they introduced their prisoners to Frenchie.

Gil got a touch of satisfaction out of the fear in the two men's eyes as Frenchie lifted them bodily and none too gently, into the back of his freight wagon.

Then, and only then, did Gil allow himself to admit the fear he'd felt at knowing he might not get back to Judith and Anna.

Not wanting to face her while he felt so vulnerable, he told Buck he would check out the spot where they would spend the night.

He returned to the wagon train half an hour before they would stop and rode beside Warren's wagon. To his surprise, Mary Mae drove it.

"Where's Warren?" he asked.

"Some problem back at the freight wagons. One you might know something about. Seems two criminals have joined our midst and were kicking up a fuss."

"Where's Anna and Judith?"

"She and Donna Grace are out walking." She pointed to the right and he saw them a distance away near the Plum Buttes. He rode over.

Anna saw him first and hollered, "Papa."

Judith turned and watched him approach. He couldn't read her expression except to note that she didn't seem too welcoming.

He swung from his saddle.

"I'll leave you two alone," Donna Grace said, and with her baby cradled in a sling across her front, she hurried away.

Judith held Anna's hand to keep her from following and waited for Gil to come closer. She studied him from top to toe. "Buck said you weren't hurt, but I'm relieved to see it for myself."

"I should have known the news would make its way throughout the train." He hadn't wanted her to know. Didn't want her to worry. And yet it pleasured him some to know she did.

"I'm just glad you're safe." She shuddered. "It could have turned out so much differently."

He removed his hat and held it with both hands at his chest. "God watches over us or none of us would safely make this trip." He tossed his hat aside, closed the distance between them and wrapped his arms around her. "My biggest concern was I might not get back to you and Anna."

Anna clung to his leg.

Judith's arms circled his waist, her face pressed to his shoulder. "I was so scared when I heard what happened. And then not to be able to see you for half the afternoon." She shuddered. "Would it have hurt you to let me know you were okay?"

"Buck surely informed you."

"All Buck said was everything was okay. The man could get an award for the way he saves words."

Gil chuckled at her tone. "Not much point in saying anything when there's nothing to say."

She leaned back. "Two captives and from what I hear, one dead man. You call that nothing?" She pulled him to the ground and they sat side by side, Anna playing at their feet.

"Tell me all about it."

Not wanting to frighten her, he sketched out the scene in a few words. "I almost missed the little hole in the wall. I believe God directed me to it."

"I'm grateful He did. I have no desire to be a widow at my age." She rested her head against his shoulder and he rested his cheek against her hair.

This was what he wanted. A woman who cherished him. He would have said more, shared from the fullness of his heart, but he had decided to court her and win her heart and he wasn't one to rush ahead of himself.

Besides, he enjoyed the thought of many special moments shared with her.

This was just the beginning of that process and he meant to make the most of it.

13

The wagons rumbled onward but Judith did not want to end this moment with Gil. She'd been glad to visit with her sister-in-law, but now she wished she could stay there with him for a long time.

Oh, how she'd worried and fretted when she heard about the prisoners in one of the freight wagons. Warren had said they were a rough pair threatening all sorts of evil upon their captors.

"Three against one," Warren had said. "It's amazing that Gil escaped with his hide in one piece."

But no one said for certain his hide was unharmed. The men dismissed the incident as simply part of an ordinary day on the trail. The women shared her concern but could offer no reassurances because Gil had ridden away without allowing Judith the chance to make sure he was okay.

And now he sat beside her, whole and unharmed and she didn't want to let him go.

His horse waited, shifting from foot to foot as if impatient.

She wanted to scold the animal and tell him to settle down, tell him Gil was staying with her so the horse might as well go find something else to do. Of course, she didn't. Wouldn't Gil think her foolish if she did? But she was happy enough to sit with his arm about her shoulders and with his cheek pressed to her hair. Only the passage of the slow moving wagons made her accept that they must move.

Gil got to his feet and pulled Judith to hers. She held Anna while he took the reins of his horse and hand in hand, they followed after the wagons, catching up as they circled near the foot of three buttes.

"They're known as Plum Buttes," Gil explained. "Those bushes circling the buttes are wild plums."

Judith looked at the bushes with interest, her mouth watering at the idea of fresh fruit. "Will there be any still on the bushes?"

"The season is over," he said.

"Wouldn't hurt to look."

He swung her hand and grinned. "I'll take you there. How would you like that?"

"I'd like it very much." Something about the gleam in his eyes made her lower her head.

They passed the wagon where the man Gil had told her about—Frenchie—lifted out the two prisoners.

Judith watched with satisfaction as Frenchie tied

them by the ankles and secured them to the nearest wagon wheel, ignoring the dire threats the men yelled.

Frenchie straightened and jammed his large fists to his hips. "Got some stinky old socks I can stuff in your mouths if you don't keep quiet." His voice was loud and with his French accent, carried the hint of a threat.

The two men swallowed back their words.

Judith waited until they were out of earshot to laugh. "You say Frenchie is a gentle giant?"

"He is."

"He sure looked foreboding to me. I could almost feel sorry for those men." Her words grew hard. "Almost, but not quite." She hadn't forgotten that they would have killed Gil if he hadn't outsmarted them.

Gil squeezed her hand gently. "Don't be wasting your thoughts on them."

"I won't." They reached the smaller camp where the passengers gathered.

Gil dropped her hand. "I'll see you later." He went in the direction the men had taken the animals. Her gaze followed him until he disappeared from view. Then she joined the other women in preparing food for tonight and for the noon meal tomorrow.

"I promised Gil an apple pie," she announced.

Three women straightened to regard her. It wasn't as if she hadn't helped with the meals since the beginning of the journey so they needn't look so surprised.

Then she realized why they had reacted that way. They cooked for the entire crew—her brothers, the

Clark sisters though one was now Mrs. Russell, and the Sheptons. Usually Polly and her uncle Sam, joined them. But Judith hadn't said she would make pie for everyone. She'd only mentioned Gil.

Mrs. Shepton recovered first. "Pie sounds delightful."

Judith set dried apples to soak while she prepared pie crust using the flour and lard they had in their supplies. Sugar was limited but she sweetened the apples enough to make them passable and filled the crusts. She made enough for two Dutch ovens so everyone could enjoy the dessert and she covered the cast iron pots with hot coals to bake.

As the women worked, they questioned Judith about her absence.

Did she find it lonely?

She let them believe she did although she'd quite enjoyed Gil's company and sharing Anna's care.

Had they had enough food?

They would have had to ask for more of the basics if their isolation had gone on much longer.

Did Anna seem to be adjusting to her situation as an orphan with new parents?

Judith gladly told them of how Anna had started to call them mama and papa.

How did she like married life?

Rather than answer, she asked Donna Grace about the baby. "How is she doing?"

Ten-year-old Polly joined them as Donna Grace explained how happy she was that the baby had decided to sleep four hours at a stretch during the night.

"Can I play with Anna?" Polly asked.

Hearing her name, Anna looked at the older girl, seemed to take measure of her then offered her a rock she had clutched in her hand.

"I'll make sure she doesn't wander away," Polly, said and the two of them began to search for rocks.

Judith smiled as she watched them. "It will be good for Anna to have company."

Mary Mae joined her in watching the girls. "It will be good for Polly too. Poor child gets lonely."

They left the girls to play and turned back to meal preparation. The others talked as they worked. Judith mostly listened, wondering how long it would be before Gil returned.

She heard the voices of her brothers and strained for a sound of Gil. Sam, Polly's uncle, followed the other men. He checked to see where Polly was before he sat down.

Gil came around the wheel of the nearest wagon. "Do I smell apple pie?" he asked.

Mary Mae answered. "Judith said she'd promised to make you one. Don't worry," she said to the other men. "She made enough for us all."

Warren and Luke nudged each other and chuckled.

Judith's cheeks grew hot and she kept her attention on the food preparation lest anyone notice. She knew the minute Gil slipped closer to the fire to warm his hands. When she stole a glance at him, she saw he watched her. His smile was a secret between the two of them, and his eyes told her he was pleased to know he'd get his apple pie.

Reverend Shepton stood to ask the blessing. His words of thanks for the health of Judith, Gil and Anna and their return to the wagon train warmed Judith's insides.

She helped serve the food around the circle. Anna sat at Gil's feet waiting to be fed. An open spot next to Gil seemed to be for her so she sat at his side.

He shifted slightly so their arms brushed.

If anyone else noticed Judith thought it nice of them not to mention it.

The conversation focused on general things—the weather that had a cold sting to it especially at night, the fate of the two prisoners though because of Polly's keen interest that subject was quickly abandoned, and then talk turned to plans for the future.

Now that Luke and Donna Grace were married and had a baby, Luke didn't plan to be on the trail any longer. He'd sell this bunch of goods and as soon as it was safe to travel over the mountains, head for California.

"We'll settle down and have a nice home," he said, putting his arm about Donna Grace and smiling at her so adoringly that Judith had to look away.

It was what she wanted. Had always wanted. She thought she'd lost the possibility when Frank died. Now she'd been offered another opportunity for it.

But could she accept it without finishing the task that sent her on the trail?

She realized the plates were clean and expectant faces turned toward her. "Who wants pie?" She jumped up to serve portions to everyone, glad of a distraction from the direction her thoughts had gone.

Gil made appreciative sounds as he tasted the pie. "Can't remember having better," he said.

The others also thanked her for the dessert.

She felt Luke's gaze on her. What did he have in mind that he wore a teasing grin? She met her brother's eyes with a silent challenge.

He grinned wider as if to inform her he meant to ignore her warning. "As long as I can remember, Judith liked to play house. She followed Ma around begging to help with everything. I think she baked her first pie—pumpkin, if I remember—when she was about eight. Isn't that right, Warren?"

Warren chuckled. "Remember how we teased her that she must have put salt in instead of sugar?"

Judith gave her brothers a dismissive wave. "You were so immature."

The others laughed.

Gil leaned closer to whisper. "Now I understand why you are so patient."

That brought a burst of disbelieving laugh from her brothers. Luke waved a finger at Gil. "She's just on her best behavior. Wait until you make her angry." He gave an exaggerated shudder.

Warren looked thoughtful. "I'd forgotten how she

liked to play house. Remember the doll house we made for her when she broke her leg?"

"Pa made it. You two only helped."

Polly leaned forward, wanting to speak.

Judith turned to her. "What is it?"

"You broke your leg?"

"I did and my papa made me a doll house to help pass the time." She met first Warren's and then Luke's gaze, as the three shared the sadness of that event.

Gil squeezed her hand, offering his sympathy.

Polly wanted to say more so Judith turned to her.

"A big doll house?" Polly asked.

"It was about this tall." Judith held her hands about three feet from the ground. "It had three bedrooms in the top and on the bottom floor, it had a kitchen, a living room and an entry way. I played with it for years." She grew thoughtful. "I expect Ma still has it stored away somewhere."

"Did you have dolls that fit?" Polly could barely sit still in her eagerness to hear all about Judith's doll house.

"I had paper dolls. Lots and lots of them. There were baby ones, boys and girls, a mama and a papa and a set of grandparents."

Polly sighed. "That would have been so much fun."

Sam pulled Polly to his lap. "I'm sorry you don't have dolls and doll houses to play with. Maybe someday we'll settle down and have a real house and you can have your own dollhouse."

Polly patted her uncle's cheeks. "It's okay, Uncle. I would sooner be with you. It's fun being on the trail."

Judith gripped Gil's hand. Polly might be happy enough with the life she shared with her uncle, but she deserved more. Just as Gil wanted more for Anna than a life of constant travel.

The pie was gone, the coffee pot drained. The men left to tend to chores and the women gathered up the dirty dishes. Judith washed. Mary Mae dried. Mrs. Shepton put beans to cook and Donna Grace fed the baby then mixed up biscuits for the noon meal tomorrow. Anna played with Polly.

Judith looked about. It might not be a house with rooms and windows, but she couldn't ask for a better family. It really wasn't so bad to be on the trail.

She finished the washing up and saw Gil lounging against a wagon wheel. He straightened. "Would you ladies be so kind as to take care of Anna? I promised Judith I'd show her the buttes."

"Anna will be fine," Mrs. Shepton said.

Judith ignored the knowing looks Donna Grace and her sister shared, but knew her hot cheeks would have shouted her embarrassment if anyone had cared to take note.

"I'll need a shawl." The evenings were cold enough to make a warm wrap and a hot fire welcome. She went to the back of the wagon where all her things had been transferred and got her shawl.

Gil waited and pulled her arm through his. "To make sure you don't stumble," he said when she gave him a questioning look. Not that she minded. In fact, she might like it a bit too much, but even so, she didn't withdraw. After all, she didn't want to fall on the rough ground and risk hurting herself. Indeed, she better hang on a little more firmly.

They left the circle of the wagons and crossed the prairie toward the buttes. The sun had dipped toward the west, throwing long shadows across the land. Her shadow and Gil's were tall and spindly and she laughed as she pointed it out.

Gil chuckled and waved his hat at his shadow.

It might be silly play, Judith thought, but it didn't hurt to be a little lighthearted.

The sound of Frenchie scolding the prisoners followed them and then the mournful notes of the harmonica came. A happy song soon replaced the sad one and she knew if she turned around she would see at least two of the teamsters dancing a jig.

"Why does the harmonica player always start out with a sad tune?" she asked Gil.

"Pete. He says one must acknowledge both sides of music. He says to play only happy tunes is to invite a reason for sadness so he gives honor to the possibility of sadness in the hopes of keeping it at bay."

The ground began to rise before them and he let her arm drop in order to take her hand and lead her up the slope. They found a path through the bushes. She pulled on his hand to slow him. "Let me see if there is any fruit." She examined the bushes and found only dried up berries.

"Too bad. It would be nice to have fresh fruit."

"They say California has all sorts of fruit. Like the garden of Eden."

"Good. Luke and Donna Grace will do well out there." She guessed Gil had more in mind than her brother and his wife, but they had agreed not to discuss that topic until they reached the end of the trail.

They continued on their way, the angle of the hill increasing. She was grateful for Gil's help.

And then they reached the crest and looked down on the landscape. The canvas on the circled wagons looked like white sails. No wonder they called them prairie schooners. Far to the east she saw a brown mass.

"What's that?"

"Buffalo."

She gasped. "There must be hundreds of them." She watched the distant animals for a few minutes then continued her examination of the land before them. In the distance she saw the reflection of water. The sun slowly made its way toward the horizon and as they stood there, gold, orange and red banners filled the sky. "It's beautiful." She'd seen lots of sunsets, and as many sunrises since they'd set out but this one was different. Where they stood gave them a wide view.

Gil stood behind her, his hands on her shoulders. She lifted her hands to his and he caught them and held them. Perhaps sharing the sunset with Gil this way also made it different.

They stood like that while the sun descended out of sight, throwing color to the sky in its wake. She would have remained staring at the sky until the last vestige of color had vanished but Gil's hands slipped down her arms and he turned her to face him.

"I've seen hundreds of sunsets but this one was special."

She was about to ask why but the warmth in his eyes stalled her words on the back of her tongue.

"It's all the more beautiful because I shared it with you." His voice deepened, the sound rumbling inside her chest.

She couldn't tear herself from the look in his eyes, realized they'd captured the gold of the sunset. He was a man with strong features, but never before had she noticed how that strength promised tenderness and protection and maybe several other things.

His gaze dropped to her mouth.

Was he about to kiss her? Her heart bounced inside her chest as if anticipating pleasure.

But with a gentle smile, he took her by the hand. "We need to get back before it's too dark to see the trail."

He was right, of course. But still, she regretted the necessity of ending the evening so soon.

Gil wanted to stay on the hilltop, Judith in his arms. He longed to claim a kiss and had every right as her husband. But he wanted something more enduring than one evening. He wanted her full-hearted loyalty. Not just a promise that he knew she would keep in her own way, but the sort of loyalty that would cause her to forsake everything else for him.

They headed back down the hill. He held her hand to keep her from falling.

"I see a rock Anna would like." Judith pulled away.

He turned to watch her pick up a rock from beside the trail. As she returned to the path, her foot caught on a tangle of grass. He knew before it happened that she couldn't regain her balance and he reached out to catch her.

The force of her body slamming into him threw him backward. He fell to his back, his arms holding Judith. She lay across his chest.

She lifted her head and looked into his eyes, hers wide with shock. "I'm so sorry. Are you okay?"

Laying there with her in his arms, he was better than okay. "I think I'll survive."

Her gaze held his. He watched the emotions in them shift from shock and worry to awareness of her situation.

He looked deep into her eyes. It was as if the fall had broken down walls in her heart and he let himself believe he saw longing for love and home. The very things he wanted. That thought might have been triggered by what her brothers had said but it didn't matter. He saw what he saw. Knew what he knew.

He tightened his arms about her and lifting his

head, caught her lips in the kiss he'd been wanting. Her lips were warm and welcoming and he lingered even as he knew it was too soon to think she would be ready to forsake everything to be his wife.

Another second of enjoyment then he shifted from under her and helped her to her feet. "Are you hurt?"

She seemed to spend longer than necessary dusting her skirt. "No, I'm fine." Her hands slowed and she straightened, her eyes filled with concern. "Are you hurt?"

"I'm fine." Though a little impatient. Something he must keep in check.

He took her hand and continued down the hill. They skirted the freight wagons where Pete still played the mouth organ, and returned to the smaller camp where a warm fire burned.

They joined the others.

Anna ran to them. She'd been prepared for bed. Someone had tried to tame her wild fair hair but it sprang into the customary fuzz about her head.

Gil's heart overflowed with love for the child and he brought her to his knee and kissed the top of her head, surprised to discover a sting at the back of his eyes.

Judith jerked as if something had hit her. "I just thought of something."

Everyone turned toward her.

The words spilled from her mouth. "Those two—" She gestured over her shoulder. "They might know

Frank's stepbrother. I need to ask them." She was on her feet in an instant.

Gil and her brothers also bolted to their feet. Anna giggled at being jostled.

Warren spoke first. "That's why you came with us? To find some relative of Frank's. If I'd known that…" He didn't need to finish his sentence in order for everyone to understand he wasn't pleased with this turn of events.

Luke looked equally displeased. "I thought you wanted to forget Frank. What's this about a step-brother?"

Gil looked from Judith to her brothers. She hadn't told them her true reason for coming with them?

Judith ignored her brothers and looked toward the other campfire. "I'm going to ask them."

"Wait a minute," Luke said.

"No, you're not," Warren said, his words an order.

Judith acted as if she hadn't heard and continued walking.

"Take her." Gil handed Anna to Mary Mae and strode after Judith. "I'm going with you."

She didn't slow her steps. "You don't want to be involved with my search for Mr. Jones."

"I didn't say that."

"But you did. And I agreed I wouldn't talk to you about it anymore. But I didn't say I wouldn't talk to others." Determination filled her voice and made her footsteps pound across the grass.

"I'm not letting you talk to them alone."

"Do as you please."

He wished she might have sounded a little more welcoming, but whether or not she wanted him to accompany her had no bearing on his decision. He would not let her talk to those ruffians alone. More than that, he wanted to know if they had any knowledge of this man.

Pete stopped playing music at their approach and all eyes turned toward them.

The prisoner who claimed to have the name Captain, laughed. "Now this is the kind of entertainment I can enjoy."

Gil placed himself protectively between Judith and the pair.

The second man who seem appropriately named Sly, leaned forward with a nasty leer upon his face.

Gil took a step toward the man, his eyes narrowed and his fists curled at his side.

Sly sat back and his leer disappeared.

The other men watched, no doubt wondering why Judith made her way toward the prisoners.

She stopped a few steps from them. Gil stayed close to her side. He didn't want her there at all but she was too stubborn to listen to his objections.

"Have you men been riding back and forth long?"

Captain looked at her like she spoke a different language.

"She wants to know how many years you've been out along the Santa Fe Trail." Gil hoped his tone of voice informed them he wanted some straight answers.

Captain's smile showed a jagged row of yellowed teeth. "What business is it of hers?"

"Answer the lady," Gil growled.

"Haven't bothered to keep track. Me and Sly just come and go as we please."

Frenchie roared with laughter. "You no go anywhere." He took a threatening step toward the pair who watched him warily. "Now answer the lady's question."

"I just want to know if you've ever met a man by the name of Jones." She spoke calmly enough but Gil heard the thread of fear in her voice and he stood closer to her.

"Jones? Last name or first name?" Sly asked, his glance going to Frenchie as if to see if the big man approved.

"Guess it could be either," Judith allowed.

Sly looked at Captain. "You ever hear tell of a Jones?"

Captain shook his head. "Don't go round gathering up names."

"Answer the lady." Frenchie curled his fists tight enough to make his knuckles pop.

"Take that as no," Captain said.

"You answer too, Sly," Frenchie said.

Sly answered hurriedly. "Never heard of a Jones."

"Thank you." Judith looked toward the drivers. "Have any of you heard of a man called Jones?"

One after another, they shook their heads or murmured, "No. Sorry."

She headed back to the others with Gil keeping at her side.

Warren and Luke waited for her, the others watching from their places around the fire.

"What'd you learn?" Warren asked.

"They never heard of him." Judith passed them and took Anna from Mary Mae's arms. "I'll put this little one to bed. Good night everyone."

Gil couldn't let the evening end like this. The sweet moments on the butte had been swallowed up in the unsavory encounter with the two prisoners. He followed her. "I'll say goodnight to Anna."

At her name, Anna reached for him. He hugged her and kissed her.

Judith climbed into the back of the wagon. "Go to your mama." He handed Anna up. "Judith?"

"We promised we wouldn't talk about it."

Like he feared, she'd let the last few moments take over her thoughts. "I just wanted to say how much I enjoyed our walk this evening."

She blinked then a smile curved her mouth. "I knocked you off your feet."

He grinned. "You surely did and I didn't mind one bit." He met her gaze openly, letting her know exactly what he meant and had the pleasure of watching her cheeks turn rosy as if she'd captured a bit of the sunset. "I'll say goodnight. Have a good sleep, both of you." And feeling rather pleased with himself, he made his way outside the wagons where he would take a turn on guard duty.

The fires died down and the camp grew quiet except for the snores of some of the teamsters and the occasional shuffling sound from the animals. The peace and solitude gave him an opportunity to review the day's events. He found himself rather pleased. He'd escaped the three men who meant him evil. He'd enjoyed an evening of courting Judith. Having her question the prisoners had even turned out rather well when they couldn't provide her with any information about a Jones man. She was learning the impossibility of her intention of finding the man.

Yup. Things were coming together. They had many days ahead of them which he meant to use to his full advantage in winning Judith's loyalty. Surely by the time they reached their destination, she would abandon all hope of finding the man and instead choose to join him in making a home.

14

Her thoughts swirling, Judith lay beside Anna, staring up at the dark canvas. The fires had died down. The camp carried only the night sounds of men and animals. Why had no one heard of Jones? She couldn't remember if Frank had ever said exactly how long he'd been on the Santa Fe Trail, but she understood it to be two or three, maybe even four years. Surely over the course of several years someone would have heard of him.

For the first time, she allowed herself to think the disloyal thought that Frank might have been wrong about where his stepbrother was.

That left her in a quandary. Was she, as Gil suggested, chasing a shadow?

Part of her would be glad if that was the case. She could freely and happily follow her dream of a home and family. But how was she to know unless she looked?

She made up her mind. She would ask every person she saw until they reached Santa Fe where she would make further inquiries. If she did not find him there, she would abandon her quest and accept the future Gil offered.

A smile filled her heart and widened her mouth as she thought of the joyful moments on the hill and the kiss he'd given her. Sharing the present and the future with Gil might be just fine.

She listened for his breathing under the wagon then remembered they were back with the others and he had gone on guard duty. Ironic, she thought, that she was surrounded by friends and family and the teamsters and she'd never felt so alone as she did knowing Gil wasn't close by.

She slipped from the wagon early the next morning, wondering if Gil would be sleeping under the wagon. In the faint hint of dawn she saw someone was there. Not bothering to be overly quiet, she started the fire for the morning.

The roll of blankets turned. An arm appeared. She watched and waited to see if Gil emerged or would it be Luke or Warren?

The arm reached for a hat.

She grinned. She'd know that battered gray hat anywhere. Gil crawled from under the wagon and rolled up his bedding.

"Good morning," he whispered, as if he didn't want

to waken any of the others.

"Good morning to you." She couldn't get enough of looking at him as he pulled on his boots and adjusted his belt. "Coffee will be ready shortly."

The grumble and yawning of others informed her the camps were awakening.

Gil crossed to her side and brushed his knuckles across her chin. "I'll be back for coffee as soon as the animals are tended." Luke and Warren joined him and they left to get the mules. She knew her brothers would also help the teamsters with the oxen before they returned.

Baby Elena cried but suckling sounds soon replaced her cries.

"Mama," Anna called, and Judith got her from the wagon.

The others were up, and the ladies worked together making breakfast. Judith gladly accepted Polly's offer to watch Anna.

Soon the smell of frying pork and boiling coffee filled the cold air.

Mrs. Shepton shivered. "It feels like winter."

Donna Grace had joined them. "Luke says we won't likely make it across the mountains. We'll have to winter in Bent's Fort."

Judith took in the information. That meant she wouldn't get to Santa Fe until spring. With a start, she realized she hoped her quest would be over before than so she could go freely into the future with Gil.

She hadn't realized how the news affected her until Donna Grace asked,

"Do you mind so much if we have to spend the winter at Bent's Fort? I've been there. It's quite comfortable. And warm and dry which is really what matters."

"I guess I hadn't thought much about it," she managed.

"Is that coffee ready?" Gil asked.

Judith jumped at his voice. He lounged against a wagon wheel. How long had he been there? Did he hear Donna Grace's question? Not that it was anything new. She had made it clear from the beginning that she meant to get to Santa Fe. A little delay didn't change that.

Except to make it longer before she found the man or gave up her search.

She poured coffee into a cup and handed it to Gil, forcing herself to meet his gaze. Why did she feel guilty that he might have overheard the conversation?

"A few weeks delay won't change anything," he murmured.

"Of course it won't," she said with enough enthusiasm to cause him to raise his eyebrows.

The other men joined them and Judith gratefully turned her attention to breakfast.

Buck rode by as they finished. "Let's roll out."

A scurry of activity followed his order. Warren called to her. "You're riding with me." She looked about. Luke and Donna Grace were in one wagon, the

Sheptons in theirs, Mary Mae rode with Sam and Polly. There was no sign of Gil.

He had gone scouting. Before they married, he rode away every morning, returning for supper, or sometimes late at night after they'd bedded down, occasionally he didn't return at all. She'd given it little thought at the time. Perhaps she'd hoped things would change now that he was a husband and a father but of course, they wouldn't.

She climbed up beside Warren and settled Anna to play with her collection of rocks.

Except much had changed. She was a married woman now with a little daughter. Judith had shared a few sweet kisses with Gil and had no reason to feel guilty about it because he was her husband.

"Nice to see you happy," Warren said, and she realized she'd been smiling as she watched the passing scenery. She didn't know how to respond to his comment so said nothing and thought he had said all he intended to say until he spoke again after a goodly time.

"You were sad a long time with Frank."

"You mean after he died."

"That too. But you didn't seem all that happy to me when you and Frank were together."

She stared at her brother. "I was very happy. We were to marry and live in that house behind the lawyer's office. I spent hours thinking how I would decorate it and what flowers I would plant."

"You always did like to play house."

"I wasn't just playing house. I was planning a home and family." How could her brother have thought she was only playing? As if her life was nothing but giant dollhouse.

"Frank seemed restless to me. That's all I'm saying."

"You've said enough." She grasped her hands together in her lap until they hurt from the pressure she exerted on them.

"I didn't mean to make you angry."

"Well, you have." He made it sound like Judith had her head so completely full of dreams that she made up the love she and Frank shared.

They rode on in sullen silence for the better part of an hour. Judith had never been able to stay angry long and the effort to do so began to wear on her nerves.

"I'm sorry I didn't tell you that I came on the trail in the hopes of finding Frank's stepbrother."

"Why is it so important to find him?"

She would not tell him any details. He likely thought Frank's death had been accidental. What's more, she was tired of having someone—namely, Gil—try and convince her not to pursue her plan. "I have a message I need to deliver to him."

Again Warren fell silent. Again, he waited a good long time before he spoke on the matter. "Is this message of life and death importance?"

She couldn't answer. When they left Independence, she would have said so. Now she was willing to give her search a true effort but accept defeat if she must.

Warren didn't say anything more on the subject

and they settled for discussing their folks and wondering how they were doing.

Buck called for them to stop for the noon break. The cold meal didn't take long to eat. The teamsters stretched out and slept as did the men of the smaller camp.

The last thing Judith wanted was more sitting, or sleeping, and she took Anna by one hand, Polly took Anna's other hand and they walked on the prairie.

Judith cupped her hand over her eyes and studied the distance. Where was Gil? When would he come back?

"Look," Polly called. "It's a dog city."

Before them lay mound after mound of dirt, the mounds more or less the size of a shopping basket.

"I've never seen anything like it," Judith said.

"Prairie dogs live here. If we're quiet we'll see them."

Sure enough in a moment an animal much like a rat poked its head from a hole then emerged. Soon there were a dozen or more standing on their hind quarters watching the intruders.

Anna chattered something and the animals disappeared so quickly that Judith laughed.

The wagons rumbled into action behind them and they hurried back.

Anna needed her nap, otherwise Judith would have been content to walk for a few hours. Maybe she'd even catch sight of Gil riding nearby.

Warren waited for her to climb into the wagon with Anna then they were on their way again.

While Anna slept, Judith sat near the back, watching the wagons behind them and often shifting her gaze to either side. She couldn't help think of the danger Gil had ridden into the previous day and sent up frequent prayers for his safety.

When Anna wakened, they joined Warren on the seat. "Are you going to keep on freighting now that Luke is headed west to start a ranch?"

"I was freighting before he joined me. Don't see any reason to quit."

The death of his wife and child had sent him away from home into this freight business. She wished for words to tell him how sad she was at his loss. And not just for his sake. She missed them too. But she knew her brother didn't care to talk about it.

Anna stood at Judith's knees and babbled about something. The only word she understood was, "Papa."

Judith pulled the baby to her lap. "Your papa is out there riding his horse." She pointed beyond the wagons to the distant horizon.

Anna leaned away from Judith. "Papa."

"Your papa will come back." But she understood how Anna would miss Gil. For a week, he'd been with them all day, every day. Judith missed him too.

In fact, by the time they circled the wagons for the night, her missing had grown into an ache. She continued to pray for his safety, but now added a plea for him to join them for supper.

The meal was ready when her prayers were answered and he rode to the camp. He swung from his saddle. Before he reached the ground, Anna squealed her delight.

"Papa, papa," she called, toddling toward him.

He caught her and swung her in the air then settled her on his hip. "Someone's glad to see me."

Judith wasn't about to race across the grass and throw herself into his arms though the temptation to do so was great. She hoped he would see the welcome in her eyes.

"You're right on time for supper," she said.

"I aimed to be." Their gazes caught and held. She didn't know how long she stared at him, unaware of anyone else until Luke cleared his throat rather loudly. She jerked her attention back to her work and was relieved when Reverend Shepton stood to say grace. A moment of closing her eyes gave her time to gather her wits.

Mealtime was the usual noise of conversation and hustle of passing food. Gil sat close to Judith, Anna at their feet. For her part, Judith cared only that Gil had returned.

"See any more ruffians out there?" Warren asked Gil, laughing as if it was a joke.

Judith gave Warren a squinty-eyed look to inform him it wasn't funny, but he didn't even bother to look her way.

"Not today. But I did find a varmint of sorts."

Her insides knotted a dozen different ways.

"What sort?" Luke asked.

She understood the men enjoyed making this into a little game, but it wasn't one she enjoyed.

"A big old rattler."

Judith shuddered. "I hate snakes."

Gil's laugh was soft and intimate. "I know." His next words included everyone. "I brought back a trophy." He dug in his pocket and pulled out a rattle and shook it.

Judith shuddered again. "I hope you made sure it was good and dead before you took those."

"It was dead. Maybe not as dead as the one you killed."

She groaned. Too late to warn him how much enjoyment her brothers would get out of teasing her.

Warren and Luke leaned forward. "She killed a snake?" Luke said.

"But how? She's deathly afraid of them," Warren added.

Donna Grace reached over and squeezed Judith's hand. "I don't blame you."

"We have to hear this story," Luke said. "Tell us."

Gil told how he had found her with the snake beaten to a pulp. "She said she wanted to teach it a lesson." His soft laugh and gentle smile filled her with satisfaction that he acknowledged her strength in dealing with a snake.

"I think I made my point utterly clear. No snake is going to get the better of me." She spoke with such forcefulness that the others laughed.

The meal ended, the men went to tend the animals, check the water barrels and prepare for the night while the women took care of dishes and children.

Judith watched Gil depart with the others. Was it the last she'd see of him tonight?

GIL RELUCTANTLY WENT with the men to take care of the camp, something he had done hundreds of times without a bit of hesitation. But in those hundreds of times, he'd never left behind a pretty little wife whose heart he sought to win.

He made sure Slack was rubbed down and had plenty of grass even if it was getting dry and old. He scouted around to ensure no intruders threatened the camp. But his thoughts continually returned to Judith. He wanted to spend time alone with her.

Somehow he managed to wait until the men began to drift back to camp, leaving behind only those on guard duty. He kept his steps to his usual pace as he made his way to the fire where Judith stood, outlined by the red and orange of the flames. He paused to enjoy the scene. She turned and saw him. Her gaze called him forward.

He reached her side. "Would you care to walk with me? I have something to show you."

She nodded.

Donna Grace had heard his request. "We'll watch Anna. Go see what he wants."

Judith thanked her sister-in-law without freeing Gil from her look.

He reached out a hand to assist her past the wagons then crooked his elbow and she tucked her arm into his. He patted her hand where it rested on his arm.

She spoke first. "I hope you don't encounter too many rattlesnakes."

"Not many. I could have avoided this one but I wanted to get his rattles."

She stopped and stared at him. "You purposely went after a snake?"

He dug the rattles out of his pocket. "These are for you."

With a shudder, she drew back. "For me? Why?"

"To remind you of what a strong, resilient person you are." His voice lowered. "And maybe to remind you of the few days you and I shared on this journey." With a chuckle he added. "And to warn other snakes to stay away."

She laughed. "Put that way, I will cherish these rattles forever." She took them from his palm, shook them so they rattled then put them in her pocket. "Thank you."

"You're welcome." She looked very inviting and he would have spent the rest of the evening in that very spot but he had something he wanted her to see.

He led her onward until they reached the bank of the Arkansas and looked at the dark waters. "We are at the Great Bend. We'll keep the river to our left for a while." He indicated a grassy spot overlooking the river and they sat side by side, watching the river ripple by.

In the distance, coyotes yapped. He heard the deeper bark of a wolf and the coyotes grew silent. He didn't mention it because he didn't want Judith to worry.

The sun dipped low and they stayed there to watch the sunset.

"Look how the colors reflect in the water."

"It's beautiful. Double the pleasure."

It wasn't the reflected sunset that doubled the pleasure for Gil. It was sharing something he'd enjoy in the past with Judith.

Something about the quietness of the place made it easy for Gil to talk. "I missed you today. Guess I got used to spending the entire day with you and Anna."

"I guess I did too."

"Isn't Warren good company?" He meant to tease, but wondered if his tone conveyed a slightly lonely note.

"Warren's my brother and thinks he can tell me what to do."

He laughed, partly because he thought Warren should know his sister would do what she thought best, and partly because it sounded like she preferred Gil's company to her brother's.

"How is Anna adjusting to having so many people around?"

Judith chuckled. "She loves playing with Polly and I

think Polly likes playing with her. She treats her like a little baby and Anna goes along with it."

"A baby? Is that good?"

Judith shrugged. "Mrs. Shepton said it was only pretend. It's rather cute though. Polly makes a little bed for her and tells her to lie down and she does. Polly sings a lullaby. Poor Polly. I think she misses her mother." Judith paused. "And a home."

Gil forgot how to breathe as he considered Judith's words. Was she acknowledging that Gil was right in saying Anna needed a home, not endless life on the trail? But they had promised not to talk about it until they reached their destination. If they wintered at Bent's Fort that would be several months.

He quietly sucked in air. All the more time to court Judith.

She seemed in no hurry to leave. Nor was he. If they waited long enough—

The sky filled with honking and flapping of wings as hundreds of white geese returned to the water for the night. They settled on the river with much squawking and shaking of wings.

He felt, as much as heard, Judith gasp. They both knew enough to be quiet so as not to frighten the birds back into flight. As they watched, some of the birds tucked their heads under their wings to sleep. Others fussed about in the water.

They stayed and watched for several minutes.

In her excitement over the arrival of the birds, Judith had taken Gil's hand, her fingers warm and clinging. Did she do it only because of the birds or did she enjoy this contact with Gil?

He knew she hadn't heard the question spoken only in his heart and yet she turned, her eyes full of joy.

"What a wonderful sight," she murmured so softly her words were barely a whisper. "Thank you for showing me them." She leaned closer.

He might have accepted it as simply the need to be close enough he could hear her low voice, but based on the welcome he read in her eyes and the way her gaze dipped to his mouth and lingered there for a heartbeat he allowed himself to believe it was more.

He needed no other invitation and dipped his head to catch her lips in a gentle, lingering kiss.

With a sigh he took for pleasure she shifted so that she leaned into his chest. He wrapped his arms about her, content to remain in this spot even though the cold night air descended.

A noisy squabble erupted among the birds and both Gil and Judith turned to watch a bird fight. It ended as quickly as it began with the offended parties squawking about it.

He chuckled. "Birds are a lot like people in many ways."

She looked up at him, a smile making her look even more kissable.

A bunch of the birds rose from the water in noisy protest at their intrusion.

Reluctantly, he rose and pulled her to her feet. "You

must be getting cold." It provided an excuse to hold her close as they made their way back to the camp.

"I thought we might have missed the geese," he said. "They migrate to Mexico for the winter."

"I really enjoyed seeing them."

He was glad but he wanted more than that.

She continued. "I really enjoyed sharing the moment with you."

He looked down at her shy smile and drew to a stop. "Me too." Not wanting to be too demanding and cause her to grow wary, he resisted the temptation to kiss her again.

They rejoined the others. Anna rushed to them. Gil lifted her. He and Judith both wrapped their arms about the little girl. Gil smiled at both of them, his heart certain this was what he wanted.

How long would he have to wait before he could take Anna and Judith to a home without wheels where they could share the joys of life?

15

J udith had little time to spend with Gil the next morning. Just long enough to wave goodbye as he rode away. But she had the memory of the previous night to keep her company as she helped with breakfast, took care of Anna and joined Warren on the wagon seat. Polly had begged to ride with them. She and Anna played in the back.

How Judith had enjoyed Gil's company. Seeing the geese had thrilled her almost as much as Gil's kiss. As they hugged Anna between them last night, Judith knew she could find the fulfillment of her dreams with Gil and the baby. Finding Frank's stepbrother seemed less important with each passing day. Several times the night before she'd considered telling Gil it no longer seemed important, but she couldn't bring herself to turn her back on Frank's death as if it didn't matter.

Of course it did and she should honor it by confronting his stepbrother.

The day passed in riding on the hard wagon seat, taking the girls for a walk, and stopping at noon without any sign of Gil. Not that she mentioned it. Everyone knew he was scouting, keeping them safe.

But who kept him safe?

God did and she prayed for protection for the man who had become her husband and for whom she admitted growing affection.

They continued on their way, Anna sleeping in the back. Seeing the quilt squares Donna Grace and Mary Mae made, each depicting some aspect of the journey, Judith decided to create her own squares. Today, she worked on one with geese flying over a river. She had plans to make one with a little girl, another with a man on horseback. She chuckled softly to herself as she planned one with a snake showing its rattles. The rattles Gil had given her were in her pocket and she touched them and thought what a special gift they were.

Her thoughts returned to her former life. Frank had given her many gifts. Flowers brought in from the east, a book of poetry—she'd forgotten it in the bottom of her trunk—and just before his death, he'd given her a silk bookmark with tassels of gold cord. It remained in the book of poetry.

But none of them meant as much as the rattles in her pocket because they were common gifts from a man. The rattles of a snake were personal, represented something special—an acknowledgment of admiration from Gil.

The afternoon rolled on, wheel turn after wheel turn. She joined her brother on the seat, Polly again in the back with Anna.

"Circle the wagons," Buck called out.

It seemed earlier than normal for a stop but Judith was glad of extra time to wash a few things. Besides it was Saturday and she wanted to give Anna a good bath. She wouldn't mind one herself but the lack of privacy made it difficult and would necessitate enlisting the help of the other women. She couldn't ask that of them. She looked about at their campsite. It was then that Judith saw the mound of rock that jutted upward in the midst of prairie with not a tree or shrub or any other object within sight though the Arkansas lay some distance to the south of them.

As she stared at the rock, Gil rode to her side. "It's Pawnee Rock. Impressive, isn't it?"

"Amazing."

"If you like, I'll take you to the top this evening and we can carve our names in the sandstone."

"I'd like that." Yes, she wanted to learn more about this mass of stone, but even more, she looked forward to another walk with Gil.

"Later then?" He touched the brim of his hat, flashed a smile and sauntered away.

Her heart as light as the evening air, she turned her attention to the evening chores.

Several times she glanced up from her work and

saw Gil talking to some of the teamsters. No doubt checking on his freight wagons.

He joined them for supper and afterwards, went with the men to take care of the stock. The meal was cleaned up, meat and beans set to simmer and he still hadn't returned.

Donna Grace straightened and glanced past Judith. "Oh my," she murmured.

Judith turned to see what had Donna Grace grinning so. Gil stood before her, clad in clean clothes, his hair damp and slicked back, beads of water dripping from the ends to his shirt. His cheeks glowed and she knew he had bathed in the cold water of the river.

He pulled his shearing-lined jacket on and donned his hat. "Are you ready?" he asked, his voice hoarse as if aware of the keen interest of the ladies looking at him.

Judith had already arranged for the others to watch Anna and she now circled the fire and went to Gil's side.

"It's Saturday night so I thought I should clean up a bit," Gil said.

Judith wished she had been able to bathe but promised herself she'd wash her hair in the morning, giving it all day to dry.

They left the wagons, the sad notes of the harmonica following them as they crossed toward the dark jutting rocks. At the foot, they stopped to stare up at rugged surface.

"At the top you'll see all sorts of names carved into the rock."

Judith considered the climb. "It looks steep."

"I'll help you." He stuck his boot on a rocky outcrop and held his hand to her.

Ignoring her reluctance to tackle the slope, she grabbed his hand and let him guide her upward. At the top, she caught her breath and looked about. "What a view," she said. She could see the Arkansas to the south. To the east, the trail they had just traversed. To the west, the trail they would travel tomorrow and in every direction as far as the eye could see, the prairie stretched on and on. Something about the vastness sucked debris from her soul and allowed fresh air and hope to fill it.

Gil followed her gaze around the landscape then settled his attention on her.

She darted a look to him and then was drawn back to the view.

He stood at her side and took her hand. "Does it make you feel small?"

"Small, but also strong. It's like I am seeing a future filled with possibility." Perhaps now was the time to tell him of her decision to limit her search for Frank's stepbrother, but before she could speak of the matter, he tugged her hand.

"This is a place the Pawnee, Kiowa and Comanche tribes use as a lookout," he said.

"Is that why it's called Pawnee Rock?"

"No, it's named because of a fight between some soldiers and some Pawnee Indians."

She looked around. "Are there hostile tribes around here?"

"Haven't seen any."

She noted that he hadn't said no and she gave the surrounding land closer study.

He caught her hand. "Come on, let's carve our names on the rocks."

She saw dozens of names in the face of the sandstone.

Gil carved Gil Trapper then handed her his knife. "Your turn."

Her tongue caught at the corner of her mouth as she concentrated on making the letters for Judith Trapper. It seemed so strange not to use the name Russell. Stranger still to think of herself as married.

Done, she stood back to admire her work.

"Maybe Frank's stepbrother's name is here." Surely, amidst all the names scratched into the rock, she'd find a Jones and assure her the man actually existed.

"Go ahead and look." Gil's tone let her know he didn't care for her to do so, but she must, and she leaned over to examine carved signatures. After a few minutes, she admitted defeat. "Guess he didn't care to add his name."

She wished she hadn't looked because the sweetness between her and Gil had vanished. "I had to check."

"I know." But he didn't sound convinced.

The fact that she still searched for the man while he wanted her to forget about him hung between them like an invisible wall. She thought again of telling him she didn't intend to look for him forever, but maybe there was an easier way to restore the good will between them.

"Should we add Anna's name?" she asked.

"I'd say so." He scratched Anna below their names. Judith went to the edge of the rock to look again at the distant horizon and try and recapture the earlier feeling of strength and joy. She heard a rattling sound. Touch her pocket to quiet the rattle in her pocket.

The rattle continued.

"Don't move," Gil said in a low voice that left no doubt about her danger.

Her heart stalled. Her lungs refused to work. Despite the cold wind sweeping over the top of the rocks, sweat beaded on her forehead. She couldn't see the snake but knew it must be close enough to find her a threat and to constitute life-and-death danger to her.

Out of the corner of her eye she saw Gil dash forward, a stick in his hand. He swung the stick. Only then did she see the snake to her right. And saw Gil kill it.

Her knees melted and she sank to the ground, gasping and crying.

Gil sat beside her and pulled her to his knees holding her. "You're safe. You're okay. I've got you."

She shuddered and clung to him. "I never saw it.

What if it had bitten me?" Another shudder. "I hate snakes."

"Guess this one never got the message to stay away from you."

His droll tone surprised her and then she started to laugh. He laughed too. She laughed until her stomach hurt. They ended up lying side by side on top of Pawnee Rock looking up into the sky. Apart from the snake, Judith knew a contentment she hadn't known in a long time.

Was Warren right? Had she not been as happy as she pretended when she was with Frank? To be honest, she had never felt the sense of peace and satisfaction she knew at this moment. Frank always sought something more. A new adventure. The opportunity to be seen in public and, she admitted, to be admired. He liked new clothes. Appearances mattered a great deal. More so, she confessed, then applying himself to any sort of work. She'd thought herself generous and patient to let him take his time, to be lulled by his explanation that his shipment had been delayed. For the first time, she allowed herself doubts.

Gil turned to his side and tickled her nose with a blade of grass. "A penny for your thoughts."

"What if I think they are worth more than a penny?"

"All I have is yours. Is that enough?"

She stared into his dark, promising gaze. No fancy words. No flowery promises, but this man spoke truth from his heart and his words meant more to her than a hundred fancy ones.

"My thoughts aren't worth even a penny," she said.

"They are to me." He dropped the grass and instead, trailed his finger along her jaw line. "Tell me what you were thinking to make the skin around your eyes tighten." He rubbed the area he meant, his touch reaching deep into her being and throwing open doors of caution.

"I was thinking how much I like your gifts."

He blinked. "What gifts?"

"A rattlesnake rattle for one. Our names in the rock. And didn't you just tell me everything you have is mine? That's pretty generous."

"I wish I could give you more."

She cupped his cheek with her hand. "Like what?"

He covered her hand with his. "If I could, I would give you a house full of joy, a life of contentment and a happy family. I would give you flowers at every window and a swing on the porch. I would give you a river with crystal clear water and trees that blossomed one after another so the air around you was always filled with the perfume of a thousand blooms."

Her mouth grew so dry she had to swallow twice before she could speak and even then could barely get her voice a whisper. "Gil, that is the most beautiful thing I have ever heard. I am going to write it down so I never forget one word."

She pulled him down so she could reach his lips

with hers and offered her thanks in a warm, claiming kiss.

He settled down beside her, holding her hand and they looked to the sky. She couldn't speak for him but she looked toward a future such as he promised. After a gift such as he'd just given, she had to assure him that she shared his dreams for the future.

"Gil, I don't know if constantly flowering trees are possible, but I'll settle for a house full of joy and a happy family."

She felt him draw in a breath and hold it. Knew he tried to understand what she said.

He pushed up to his elbow. "I hope it is possible." Guessed he feared to make too much of it.

She understood that he didn't believe she would abandon her search for Frank's stepbrother. But she would once they'd reached Santa Fe. Either she would have found him by then or she would no longer try and locate him. She could let it go at that point knowing she had done her best.

He got to his feet and pulled her up. "We don't want to be finding our way off the rocks after dark."

She wished he would have gone further in response to her offer, but once they started to make their way down she was glad they left when they did as the descent required searching for careful footing. She was grateful Gil held her hand and guided her down.

He was the sort of man she knew she could trust to

hold her hand and walk with her through the life he had offered.

Gil went over Judith's words again and again the next day as he watched for signs of raiders and checked for places to stop at noon and then later, to spend the night. *I'll settle for a house full of joy and a happy family.* He grinned. Could she mean it? Well, of course she did. But what exactly did she mean? She'd settle after she found the Jones guy? He'd hoped she might be willing to give up the search, but yesterday on Pawnee Rock it was clear she hadn't. She'd spent several minutes searching through the many names.

He was tired of life on the trail and wanted to settle down. There was only one thing for him to do. Help her find the Jones man so they could have their happy home and family. The only thing that bothered him about his decision was how it affected Anna. Life on the move, especially in the area Judith searched for the Jones man, was hard and dangerous. Anna deserved better and he had promised more than constant travel when he agreed to see she got a good home.

But he couldn't make a home without Judith. Home meant life shared with her. There'd be no chance to tell her of his decision tonight. They would put in a long day for their journey took them across a difficult crossing. Moreover, it was the Sabbath and Reverend Shepton would have a sermon prepared.

As he predicted, the crossing was tough. The banks were steep and required branches to be cut to stick through the spokes of the wheels to act as brakes. Then the teams had to be doubled up to pull the wagons through sand up to the hubs. The afternoon was almost spent by the time the wagons were all safely across.

Buck, Warren, Luke and Gil took stock of the situation. The men were tired. The animals exhausted and everyone wet from fighting their way back and forth across the river.

Gil gave his opinion. "We're near water, there are woods to the Southwest. I think we should spend the night here." Ahead of them were two days without a good water source. "Let the animals get their strength back and fill up with water."

Buck studied the landscape and adjusted his hat twice as he made a decision. "We'll camp over there." He pointed toward the woods.

The wagons were ordered to move that direction and then circled.

For his part, Gil thought a Sunday rest of a couple hours couldn't go wrong.

Despite his wash in the river last night, he was in sore need of another scrubbing and he went into the river, clothes and all and removed the mud and sand of the day's work.

Dripping wet, he made his way to the teamsters' fire. Not until he had dried off would he join the smaller group.

After fifteen minutes of shivering, he changed his mind and dug a change of clothes out of one of his freight wagons, put on the dry ones and hung the wet. Then he sauntered over to where Judith held Anna on one hip and stirred a pot with the other hand.

He paused to watch her, picturing her in a warm kitchen with Anna and two or three other little ones nearby. He imagined her in the house full of joy that he had offered her.

She lifted her head, saw him and smiled. He knew the promise of that joy depended on her.

He hurried to her side and took Anna from her arms. Without thinking about what he did, he leaned forward and kissed Judith's cheek which immediately flooded with color. Feeling rather pleased with his life, he sat down to play with Anna.

They ate early then Reverend Shepton called for their attention. "It's Sunday. Let's worship the Lord and thank Him for traveling mercies."

The teamsters sat quietly, happy enough to accept whatever church service was offered.

Judith sat beside Gil, Anna in his lap. She was drowsy so didn't protest at having to be still.

The reverend led them in some familiar hymns. Pete played the harmonica to accompany them, but nothing compared to hearing Judith's sweet, clear voice blend with his deeper one. He decided she shared the feeling when she sent him a little smile before turning her attention back to the reverend who spoke about Moses leading the children of Israel across the desert. He concluded with the verse, "'The eternal God is thy refuge, and underneath are the everlasting arms.'"

As the others dispersed, Gil whispered to Judith, "Was that one of the verses you memorized?"

She smiled. "That and ninety-nine others."

"It's a wonderful thing your mother had you do." He thought of the few times she had recited verses, and how the words meant so much coming from her. "I look forward to hearing all of them."

"Maybe not all at once."

He agreed, recognizing it as a promise for the future. Tomorrow, he reminded himself, he would tell her of his decision to help her find the Jones man. The sooner she found him, the sooner they could start their home together.

With Anna asleep in his arms, Gil was in no hurry to end the evening, but the other men went to tend the evening chores and he was on first guard duty so he took Anna to the wagon and bade Judith goodnight.

Reverend Shepton had reminded Gil of God's care and how He answered prayer and he prayed that they would find this Jones fellow as quickly as possible. *Perhaps before we get to Santa Fe.* If they found him in Bent's Fort perhaps they could join Luke and Donna Grace in heading west to start ranching.

He smiled as he circled the wagons doing his duty as the night guard. The future held the promise of home and family.

16

Judith barely saw Gil the next morning. He ate early then set out. Warren said water was scarce ahead and Gil had gone to scout out possible spots where they might find some.

"Otherwise we will be forced to follow the Arkansas. That route is less direct and harder travel."

"I pray for success for him." Judith didn't add that she was far more concerned with the risk of rattlesnakes, raiders, angry Indians and any number of things than whether or not they had to take the easiest, fastest route.

They nooned without any sign of Gil. She did her best to hide her concern, but perhaps not as well as she hoped for Donna Grace joined her as she looked to the west hoping to see him riding back.

"He's an experienced scout," Donna Grace said.

"Doesn't stop me from worrying."

Donna Grace chuckled. "One of the perils of love."

Judith was about to deny love had anything to do with it, but stopped herself. Let her sister-in-law think what she would. But as she turned her attention to other things, she considered the assumption. She'd grown fond of Gil, looked forward to the day they could make a home together, and missed him so much it hurt when he was away. Was that love?

She sat on the wagon seat beside Warren as they continued. The afternoon grew unbearably hot. "How can it be so cold at night and so hot in the day?" She wiped sweat from her brow and wished they were closer to the river. A dip in its cold waters sounded mighty enticing at the moment.

Warren studied the sky, a worried frown on his face.

"What's wrong?" She looked at the sky too but saw nothing. A few clouds to the west but that wasn't unusual. In fact, they were quite beautiful with the sun's rays poking through. Like the fingers of God, she thought.

"I don't like this weather. It's too hot for this late in the year."

She'd never considered her eldest brother to be a worry wart and his concern sent trickles of tension through her. She rehearsed all the disasters bad weather could bring.

If only Gil would return.

To calm her fears, she mentally quoted the Twenty-third Psalm. Peace returned, especially when she thought of how much Gil like to hear her say her memorized verses.

Over the rattle of the wagon and the beat of the mules' hooves she heard a horse coming up beside them and turned. Gil. She almost shouted his name and stopped herself in time, offering a welcoming smile instead. Had he come to tell them they would soon stop for the night? She hoped so. Maybe he would ask her to walk with him again. He might even have brought her another gift and she tried to think what it might be. Perhaps a pretty rock that looked like a jewel. Or a fragrant bit of greenery.

He grinned and touched the brim of his hat in greeting.

Why did such a simple gesture turn her insides to molten honey?

He rode at her side. "Where's Anna?"

"Papa," the child called, peering out from behind Judith. Polly stood beside her.

"The girls like to play together."

"Hi girls," he said. He leaned forward in his saddle. "Hi Warren. Is everything okay?"

Warren glanced at the sky. "You tell me."

The clouds had grown dark and heavy. Lightening flashed in the distance and thunder echoed. Too far away to be of any concern, Judith wanted to say, but the worry on both men's faces made her wonder if they knew something she didn't.

"We could be in for a soaker," Gil muttered.

"Or worse," Warren said.

"You guys are making me nervous. Why would a little rain bother us?"

"Hopefully it won't. I'm going to check on the wagons." Gil rode down the line.

Judith turned to her brother. "What are you concerned about?"

"Storms out on the prairie can be unpredictable."

She understood that but they had ridden out several storms already and apart from the rain and wind, it had been bearable. A wind tugged at her clothes. The heat she'd recently complained about vanished. She shivered and reached behind her for a shawl. "Are you girls warm enough?"

Polly nodded. "We'll make a tent of the blankets if we get cold."

Dark clouds raced toward them with lightning and thunder coming from the swirling midst.

Warren's grasp on the reins tightened.

"Are they going to bolt?"

"Not if I can help it." But the mules skittered as lightning flashed so brightly that Judith found herself momentarily blinded. Then thunder roared.

"Mama," Anna cried.

"Stay with Polly. Polly, wrap her up and hold her."

The lightning flashed so close that Judith wondered if they would be struck. They were the highest objects in the wild, flat prairie.

She wondered why they didn't stop for the night and circle the wagons.

Thunder snapped close on the heels of each flash. The air filled with static and the smell of gunpowder.

"Something's been hit," Warren said and turned the wagon about to look behind them.

Flames lit the canvas of one of the wagons.

Buck rode down the line. "Pull out. Secure your wagons and find something to fight fire with."

Now she understood why they hadn't stopped. Fire could easily go from one wagon to another if they had circled.

Warren was on the ground and grabbed the shovel. He'd secured the reins. "If the animals get too skittish take the girls and get out of the wagon. Don't try and hold them, and above all, don't stay in the wagon." He raced toward the burning wagon. Wagons had been turned aside up and down the trail and men hurried in the same direction.

She stood to better see and scanned the crowd of men. Not until she picked out Gil's gray hat could she fill her lungs. Just as quickly she stopped as Gil struggled to free the oxen from the burning wagon.

He led them away and her starving lungs sucked in air.

The fire consumed the canvas and ate at the wood. The whole load would be lost unless the men could put out the fire.

She strained to see what was going on. Was that Gil pulling things from the burning wagon? Her heart slammed into her ribs. He'd climbed into the wagon.

He threw things out. *Gil*, she silently screamed, *nothing in there is worth losing your life over.*

He jumped from the back allowing her to again feel her limbs.

Flames spread from the wagon. The prairie burned. The men swung gunny sacks or beat at the flames with shovel. The wind drove the fire at a furious rate.

A bit of burning canvas blew from the wagon and a second wagon ignited, lighting up the dark sky.

Gil waved his arms and a handful of men raced back to the standing wagons and moved them further away. A couple of men led the oxen away from the burning wagon.

The orange and red of the fire outlined the men. Judith prayed for their safety and continually sought for a glimpse of the gray hat. *Please keep him safe.*

The prairie fire continued to spread and the men continued to run ahead of it and attempt to beat it out.

If only the wind would go down or the clouds would open and send rain. *Please, God, make one or both happen.*

Lightning continued, the flashes turning the scene into a silver and red picture.

Another flash. Thunder instantly following. The mules stomped and yanked at the reins. She had no wish to be in a runaway wagon. "Polly, we're leaving the wagon. Take Anna to the back." As she spoke, she jumped from the wagon and raced around to take Anna. Polly jumped down without any urging.

Judith led them a goodly distance from the wagon to a spot where she felt safe, but could still watch the men. She barely looked away when the wagon she had so recently vacated raced away. The evening had closed in about them.

The second wagon burned unabated. They should have stayed close to the river where they could get water to fight the fire. But it was too late to change what was.

She sank to the ground, holding Anna tightly. Polly pressed to her side.

"Is my uncle okay?" Polly asked.

"The men are careful. They won't do anything that might put them in danger." She kept part of her attention on the spreading grass fire. Where would she go if it came toward her? Should she go toward the river? It was some distance off. Perhaps she should head that direction now. She glanced around to see where the other women were. Through the smoke billowing about them, she thought she made out the wagons to the north. Perhaps she should join them. But she didn't move in either direction because she couldn't take her eyes off the fire and the men fighting it.

"He won't let his wagons burn." Polly's voice carried the threat of tears. "He says we'll soon stop traveling the trail and get us a real home. He says I'll be able to have my own dog and not have to share like I do with Mister King."

Judith knew she referred to the camp dog she had given that name to. Seems many of the men were growing tired of their wandering lives and looking forward to having a home.

The men gathered at the leading edge of the grass fire beating out the last flames. Good. They'd stopped it. They remained there, watching for flare ups while the two wagons slowly burned into the ground.

Gil crossed the blackened area and went to the smoldering wagons. Nothing in either of them would be worth salvaging. It would be a great loss for the owner.

The teamsters remained at the site of the fire to make sure the wind didn't fan it into flames. Luke came through the smoke and found his wagon with Donna Grace and baby Elena.

Reverend Shepton, his steps slow and heavy, made his way to his wife in their wagon.

Polly saw Sam and raced toward him. He caught her and hugged her close then they turned aside.

Warren stood near the smouldering wagon, Gil at his side.

She sat motionless and waited for Gil.

Warren and Gil finally left the scene. Fifty yards from where she sat, they stopped. Only then did she remember the mules had run off with the wagon. They would be wondering what happened to her.

She stood and called.

Gil saw her in the dusk and ran to her. He caught her to him, Anna between them.

Judith breathed in the acrid smell of smoke. "I'm so glad you're safe," she murmured.

"You gave me a fright when I didn't see you at first."

Warren stood nearby. "The wagon?" he asked.

She pointed the direction the mules had gone, and Warren went after them.

Judith could not ease her hold on Gil even though Anna squirmed and protested.

Gil shifted, took Anna in one arm and held Judith tight to his other side. She wrapped her arms about his waist and wondered if she would ever be able to let him go.

"Whose wagons burned?" she asked.

"Mine."

"Both of them?" Shock made her voice thin.

"Both of them." He sounded weary clear through.

"Oh Gil, I'm so sorry. But at least you're safe."

Warren returned with the wagon. Gil released her and handed her the baby. She wished she could have kept her arms around him.

"I have to help Buck get the camp organized and look after my oxen."

She let him go, although every thought rebelled at having to do so. Two wagons was a great loss, but he was alive and well. That was all that mattered to her.

How much did the loss mean to him? She couldn't help but think of Frank, and how his loss had meant more to him than she did.

But Gil wasn't like that. She was wrong to let the idea enter her mind.

They circled the wagons and made camp. The wind had subsided and the storm moved off, but smoke from the two burned wagons drifted toward them.

Judith helped with camp chores, but her thoughts were on Gil. When would he come?

A horse rode away from camp. She recognized it as Gil's and he, the rider.

Despite her determination not to think it was anything like Frank, her heart sank like it was full of stone.

GIL RODE FROM THE CAMP. Buck expected him to find water and camping spots. He expected Gil to warn of any danger threatening the wagon train. He would do that but mostly Gil wanted to leave behind the destruction of two of his three wagons. He had counted on the sale of the contents to set up a fund for his stepmother to live on and another for Stu's future needs. With the rest of the money he hoped he could start a new life in the west with Judith and Anna.

He had savings. Were they enough to meet his needs? He rode to the river, dismounted and sat over-looking the water as he considered his options.

This might set him back enough that he would have to stay on the trail another year.

As he sat, he added up the numbers. Was this God's way of saying Gil should continue freighting? Perhaps his journeys back and forth would be the means of helping Judith find this Jones fellow.

His heart hurt at the thought. It wasn't what he wanted.

Maybe, on the other hand, it was God freeing from the freight business. If he sold the remaining wagon and goods and all the animals, he would have the money he needed for his stepmother, Stu and a home.

That was his answer.

He rose, feeling better than he had since he saw the fire start on his first wagon. What a sinking feeling he'd had as the second caught fire. It was like watching his dreams go up in smoke.

A smile on his face, he returned to Slack. "Except, old boy, it's no longer my dream. My dream is a home with Judith and Anna and whatever children the Lord sees fit to bless us with."

He rode toward the wagon train.

"Only one thing left to do," he informed his horse. "Help Judith find the man she seeks so we can get on with our life together."

By the time he reached the camp, the fires had died down and apart from the guards, everyone had bedded down. Rather than risk disturbing those sleeping, he took his bedroll and crawled under his last remaining freight wagon.

Tomorrow he would tell Judith his plans. Not that it changed anything for the next few weeks as they continued on their journey. But once they reached Bent's Fort he would ask around about the Jones man. He'd ask men Judith should never speak to.

The mountain pass would be closed by now. They would have to winter at the Fort.

Not something he minded contemplating.

He smiled as he thought how pleased Judith would be at his announcement.

He could only hope and pray that they would find the man. *Please God, let us find him in Bent's Fort.* That way they could continue west with Luke and Donna Grace.

Losing two of his wagons was a disaster, but not without a positive side. The loss made him see what really mattered and it wasn't the freight, being on the trail or even the money he made by selling his goods.

He knew exactly what he wanted. A home and a family with Judith and Anna.

THE SKY HAD NOT LIGHTENED when Gil woke the next morning but already men were stirring. Pete, who not only played the harmonica but made the best breakfast, arranged wood and started the fire.

The smoke from the fire of yesterday lingered in the air—an unpleasant reminder of what had happened.

He lay a moment longer in his warm bedding, grateful that the fire had not done more damage nor gotten out of control in the prairie grass.

Would Judith be up yet? He was anxious to tell her his plans.

Despite the loss of two of his wagons, they would

have a home and a family just as he had promised her and promised Anna's father.

Ignoring the cold, he slipped from his bed, rolled the bedding, stowed it in his wagon then trotted out to help the teamsters with the oxen.

"Don't hurt to have some spares," one man commented.

"They can spell off each other," another added.

Gil assured the men they would all receive their expected pay. "I'll be counting on you to get the animals safely to Bent's Fort." He knew he could get a fair price for them there.

As soon as the animals were cared for he went to the burned out wagons. As he expected there was nothing worth salvaging except for a cast iron fry pan. He took that to Pete. His gaze went to the other campfire where the women prepared breakfast.

He didn't care to share his news in front of everyone, but he couldn't put off seeing Judith and jogged over.

She looked at him and started to sob.

That was hardly the greeting he expected, and he stopped to think what was wrong.

"I didn't know if you were coming back," she managed between gulps.

"Why wouldn't I come back?"

"Frank didn't."

Not caring how many watched nor what they thought he closed the distance between them and pulled her to his chest. "Judith, I will always come back. How else am I going to keep my promise to you?"

She sniffled. "What promise is that?"

He eased her away from the others so he could speak freely. "A house full of joy, a life of contentment and a happy family." He hoped she would recall the rest. All the ways he wanted to bless her life.

"Oh, that one." She shuddered. "When you left without saying a word…"

"I regret that I caused you worry. I'll try to do better in the future. But—" He leaned back so he could look into her teary eyes. "I am not Frank. You can count on me."

She blinked back her tears and continued to look at him until she was satisfied. "Thank you."

"You're welcome." He kissed the tip of her nose.

Anna called to them and Gil laughed. "Seems our little daughter wants us. Let's join the others for breakfast." He took her hand and they went back to the fire.

No one said anything, but Donna Grace and Mary Mae both gave Judith a quick hug.

Luke and Warren studied Judith, seemed relieved that she was okay. They each gave Gil a look that warned him he better not hurt their sister. He had no intention of doing so. He smiled at them. Throughout breakfast, his smile hovered close to the surface. As soon as he got an opportunity he was going to tell Judith that he would help her find Frank's stepbrother. He watched for an opening. Perhaps he could steal her away for a few minutes and leave the others to prepare for the day's journey. But as he was about to ask, Buck rode up.

"Gil, the men could use some help with your oxen."

"I'll be right there." Gil had no choice but to leave, but then it wasn't as if he wouldn't get a chance to see Judith later. They would be on this journey together for many days yet.

The day alternately passed quickly and then slowed to a snail's pace. By the time Gil had shared supper with the group, his insides jittered with anticipation and a tiny degree of anxiety. He wasn't a man used to talking to a woman. Perhaps he wouldn't get it right.

"Would you walk with me?" he asked Judith when the meal was over and the chores attended to.

"Of course."

Mary Mae said she would watch Anna.

Gil took Judith's arm and they wandered past the circle of wagons, Pete's harmonica music accompanying them. They walked across the dry grass until they found a spot where they could watch the sunset, though that was not his reason for stopping.

Judith faced him, her hands on his upper arms. "Gil, I'm sorry you lost your wagons, but I want you to understand that the loss of income does not matter to me. I will stand by you whatever happens."

He wrapped his arms around her and touched his forehead to hers. "Judith, thank you for saying that. There is something I've been wanting to tell you."

She tipped her head back to look into his eyes, hers full of uncertainty.

"Don't look so worried. It's something you'll like. I promise." He waited until trust replaced the concern in her eyes. "That's better."

Her smile warmed his insides.

"I want you to know that I have decided I will help you find this Jones fellow and stay with you until you have found him."

She studied him, her gaze going from his one eye to the other. "Have you given up on having a home?"

"Not at all, but until you are ready for it, neither am I." He didn't mention Anna. The child would have to accompany them. "I'm hoping we'll find the man at Bent's Fort." He watched her assess the information. Why wasn't she pleased with his announcement?

A smile crept across her face. She cupped her palms to his cheeks. "Perhaps you will be happy to hear that I have also come to a decision. I will search for Frank's stepbrother only as far as Santa Fe. If we don't find him there, or before there, I will let it go."

He whooped. "Glad to hear it." He hugged her tight, his cheek resting on her head. "I'm hoping and praying we will find him at the fort so we won't have to travel further south."

"That would be nice."

He could not miss the longing in her voice and his heart swelled with joy to know she wanted the same thing he did—to move on and start a real home.

They sat on the grass, neither of them in a hurry to

return, content to be together and anticipating their future.

Judith bounced to her feet and held out a hand to him. "I have something I want to show you."

"What?" He chuckled at her enthusiasm as she tugged on his hand to hurry him back to the camp.

"You'll see in a minute. Wait here." She indicated a spot by the wagon.

No one took more than a glance toward Gil as he leaned against the wheel, listening to Judith rummage around inside the wagon. The campfire blazed, dispelling the chill of the November evening. Luke and Donna Grace sat side by side, their attention on baby Elena. Warren and Sam talked together, looking at something Sam scratched in the dirt. Polly and Mary Mae played cats-in-the-cradle with Anna watching them. The Sheptons had retired to their wagon.

"Got it." She scrambled down and came to him, holding what looked like a photograph. Two feet away, she stopped. "I don't know what I was thinking. This won't be of any help." She put her hands behind her back.

"What is it?"

"A picture of Frank. I thought it might help us find his stepbrother, but I forgot they aren't blood related."

Frank? He was curious to see what the man who had been so careless of Judith's feelings looked like. "Let's have a look."

She hesitated then nodded. "I wouldn't mind if you

saw him for yourself." She handed him the sepia-colored photograph.

He stared. Tipped the picture toward the fire to see it better and swallowed hard.

"This is Ollie."

"No, it's Frank."

He tapped the picture with his index finger. "I'm as sure as can be that this is my stepbrother, Ollie. What kind of game is this?"

17

J udith snatched the photograph from Gil and stared at him. "You're Frank's stepbrother? You stole his money? You are responsible for his death?"

"Judith?" Luke called. "What's wrong?"

Warren was on his feet and headed toward her.

She didn't want to talk to anyone and she fled to the wagon, climbed in the back and pulled the rope tight to close the opening.

"Judith?" Warren spoke from the back.

"Go away. I don't want to talk."

"Judith, it's me. Luke."

She rolled her eyes. Like she wouldn't know his voice. "Leave me alone."

Thuds of booted feet let her know they had gone. Murmured conversation reached her though she couldn't make out any words. She didn't need to. Everyone had seen her with Gil, had heard her reaction. And now they were set on reasoning with her.

Only one voice she didn't hear. Gil's. Not that she wanted to. She fell on her knees before the trunk and put the photograph back in its safe place.

How could Frank's stepbrother be Gil? Had he known all along and simply played a trick on her? How could she trust him?

She lifted the book of poetry Frank had given her from the trunk. She had trusted Frank, given him her complete loyalty. In return, he had left her as if she didn't matter in the least. And now she'd come within a hair's breadth at giving her heart completely to Gil.

At least she'd found out in time who he really was.

"Judith?" It was Donna Grace.

"I'm sorry. I need to be alone so I can think."

"I understand. I'm only here to bring Anna."

Anna! Judith couldn't believe she'd momentarily forgotten the child and she hurried to loosen the rope and take her from Donna Grace. "Thank you." Anna slept and barely stirred as Judith settled her at the end of the trunk.

She would have remembered Anna in a few minutes, but admitting she'd forgotten for even a bit made her wonder if she had a deep flaw within her. One that made her trust people she shouldn't and fail those who trusted her.

The idea made her groan. She immediately cut off

the sound knowing those outside the wagon could hear. The last thing she wanted was to have them inquiring about what was wrong.

Everything was wrong. She didn't know how to fix it. Or if it could be fixed.

She prepared for bed and lay beside Anna. But sleep would not come. Instead, a list of problems circled in her head. She was married to the very man she blamed for Frank's death. She'd allowed hate to fester toward Frank's stepbrother. She couldn't separate Gil from the man she sought. Nor did she understand how she could be so confused she didn't realize who he was. Had he changed his name to protect himself?

How was she to deal with this cruel twist of events?

She tried to calm her mind by quoting the Twenty-third Psalm, but she found no comfort in it as she recalled reciting the verses for Gil.

Morning came and with it the knowledge she would see Gil. Unless he'd left as he often did. *Oh, please, let this be a morning he is out scouting for the entire day.*

She carried Anna from the wagon and looking neither to the left nor the right, joined the ladies preparing breakfast. "Good morning." Hopefully her cheery voice would make them think she had forgotten last night, and everything was as usual.

Mary Mae and Donna Grace exchanged looks that

made Judith think they weren't as convinced as she'd like them to be. Be that as it may, she took care of Anna, baked biscuits and forced steel into her heart as the men joined them for breakfast.

Gil was with them. So much for hoping he'd be scouting today.

She carefully avoided him, choosing to sit by Polly and Sam hoping everyone would think it was because Anna wanted to be with her friend.

Gil waited a moment after breakfast was over.

She ignored him. What could she say? For that matter, what could he say?

Buck called for them to move out. Gil went to his horse and rode away. Only then did Judith relax.

She sat beside Warren on the hard bench.

He barely waited for her to get settled before he spoke. "Judith, what's wrong between you and Gil?"

"I don't want to talk about it."

"I couldn't help but overhear you accuse him of being responsible for Frank's death."

"I don't want to talk about it."

"How can you blame him?"

Had her brother gone deaf? "I don't want to talk about it." She spoke through clenched teeth.

"He's a good man."

Obviously there was no point in repeating herself again so Judith sat in silence.

"He isn't like Frank, you know."

What did any of them know if he was like Frank or not? Obviously Frank's family situation was bad enough that he left home and it seems, he even went under a different name.

Warren tried a few more times to talk to Judith but her stony silence didn't end and he gave up.

Gil didn't appear for the noon meal and for that, Judith was grateful. She chose to ride in the back with Anna for the afternoon, not asking to move to the seat even when Anna wakened from her sleep. Instead, she played with the child hoping to put her anger at bay.

Except it wasn't anger she felt though she tried to convince herself it was because it was easier to be angry at Gil, angry at herself for trusting him, angry at Frank—

She stopped. For the first time since his death she admitted she was angry at him for choosing that way out of his problems.

But toward Gil she felt only despair. It was an odd word she hadn't considered but it fit perfectly. Here she was married to a man she believed to be a cheater. Not only that, but they had a child they had planned to raise together. Moreover, she had promised him she'd be faithful. But of course, that was before she knew who he really was so her promise was null and void.

Unable to deal with the rage of emotions in her heart, she lay down, Anna playing at her side. If only—

She jerked awake at the sound of her name in Warren's voice. He seemed concerned.

"What's wrong?"

"I called your name several times and you didn't answer."

"I fell asleep."

"Where's Anna?"

The baby played in the corner, but again, Judith's mental state had caused her to overlook her duties as a mother. She pushed to her feet. "I'll ride with you."

Polly had been waiting for a chance to get in the back so she and Anna could play together. Judith thought Polly might do a better job of watching Anna than she had been doing.

They continued down the trail.

"We are about to pass the Caches," Warren said.

She could tell by the tone of his voice that he expected her to be interested and she did her best to appear so.

"A man named Beard and his fellow travellers were overtaken by winter and dug holes." He pointed toward an elevated bit of ground. "They lined the holes with moss and stored their goods there until they could return with help to retrieve them. You'll want to see them."

Luke and the reverend had turned their wagons aside and Warren followed. The truth was, Judith didn't care about holes in the ground, but the fact that the men had been overtaken by winter sent a skitter of fear through her. They were travelling late in the season. What would they do if the weather turned bad enough to prevent further travel?

She alighted with the others and exclaimed along with them, but was glad when they continued on their way.

They camped for the night further down the trail.

She'd seen nothing of Gil since breakfast and for that, she was grateful.

GIL COULD HAVE RETURNED to the others at nightfall but instead, chose to make camp a distance away. His thoughts had gone in endless circles all day long. How could Frank and Ollie be the same person? Yet there was no doubt they were. What had Frank/Ollie told Judith? Was there truth to any of his story?

Gil had been gone a long time from home. When he returned at his pa's death, he knew only that his father was deeply in debt. He'd blamed Ollie. Was he wrong? Had someone else, without his stepmother's knowledge, been involved, leaving Ollie to blame Gil? Had he been too quick to assume Ollie was the one taking advantage of their father?

WHAT REALLY HAD his mind churning was Judith's accusation that Gil was to blame for her fiancé's death. He'd hoped they would find the stepbrother she sought in Bent's Fort, but he never expected they would find him before and it would be him.

He hunkered down over his small fire. The cold of the evening matched the temperature of his heart.

How was he to go on...how were *they* to go on together...with this misunderstanding between them?

If they could talk, understand what had happened, perhaps come to a resolution—but she made it plain she didn't want to talk.

Sooner or later he would insist they must, but he'd give her time to realize on her own that he was not the scoundrel Ollie—or did he mean, Frank?—had made him out to be.

IF JUDITH THOUGHT Warren would leave off trying to discuss her situation with Gil, the next morning made her see otherwise.

"I don't want to talk about it," she insisted.

"Well, I do."

"Just because you're bigger and stronger, doesn't mean you get your own way." They had teased each other this way growing up, but she didn't feel in a teasing spirit today.

"I'm your big brother so I get to speak my mind."

She looked to the side, prepared to ignore him which was impossible when he sat only a foot away.

"Gil isn't Frank," he said.

"It appears Frank isn't even Frank." She had the satisfaction of seeing him look surprised and confused.

"What does that mean?"

She explained.

"Why would Frank lie to you?"

"I ask myself the same question."

"Seems to be this is something you and Gil need to talk about. If you compare what each of you knows about the situation you might come to some understanding."

She refrained from saying they would both have to want an understanding. But Warren was right. Something had to be resolved.

Gil didn't show up until they stopped for the night. He joined them for supper.

"We need to talk," he said when the meal ended.

"I agree." A couple of days ago she would have anticipated being alone with him, but today, her insides jumped about like water on a hot skillet.

"We'll take care of Anna," Donna Grace said and shooed Judith away.

Judith fell in at Gil's side, but kept a foot or more between them.

He stopped as soon as they were out of earshot of the wagons. "I am not responsible for Frank's death though he is my stepbrother, Ollie."

"Did you take the money he expected to get?"

"I did not get any money. I told you my stepbrother left my father penniless."

They didn't look at each other as they spoke.

"Why did he call himself Frank?"

"I thought about it. His name was Oliver Francis Trapper. Before his mother married my father his last name was Crosby. I don't know where Jones came from any more than I can say why he did this."

She considered the information. "I don't know what to think."

"That's not very encouraging. You'll have to decide for yourself if I'm the man you've seen and talked with these past few weeks or if I'm who Frank said I was."

It sounded like an ultimatum, but he was right. She had to decide who he was. It felt disloyal to Frank to cast doubts on what he'd said.

She heard Anna cry and listened. The child continued to cry. "I need to see what's wrong with her."

They both hurried back to the wagons.

Anna reached for Judith as soon as she saw her and Judith held her close.

Gil pressed his hand to Anna's head. Judith's gaze went to his and she felt a jolt of truth. One thing they were agreed on was their love and concern for this child. But was that enough?

"She kept calling for you," Donna Grace said.

"I'm here," Judith crooned to Anna.

"Both of you," Donna Grace said with some emphasis.

Luke came to his wife's side. "She knows something is wrong between the two of you and it has her upset."

"I'll put her to bed." Judith climbed into the wagon. Anna needed them together. They were married.

Anna settled, two fingers in her mouth.

Judith opened her trunk to look at Frank's picture again and try to understand who he was. Her eyes fell on the book of poetry he had given her. Not once had he read any of the poems to her.

She opened the book. In the flyleaf she had penned the words Gil had spoken to her.

If I could, I would give you a house full of joy, a life of contentment and a happy family. I would give you flowers at every window and a swing on the porch. I would give you a river with crystal clear water and trees that blossomed one after another so the air around you was always filled with the perfume of a thousand blooms.

The words were more beautiful than any of the poems in the book.

She sat back—because they were spoken from the depths of his heart revealing who he really, truly was.

Finally, her heart emptied itself of the sorrow and guilt inflicted by Frank's death. She understood now what her father and brothers had tried to tell her. Frank was not what he appeared to be.

She put the photograph back in the trunk, replaced the poetry book on top of it and closed the lid.

Anna slept peacefully so Judith left the wagon.

Gil sat hunched over the fire, silent as the others talked. She went to his side.

"We need to finish our discussion."

He jolted to his feet, a look of surprise in his eyes.

She caught his elbow and steered him away from the wagons. Darkness had fallen so she didn't go far, just far enough to ensure a bit of privacy. She stopped.

"I've had time to think."

He didn't answer, but she could feel him tense.

"Frank was not what he pretended to be. I should have seen it sooner. He had a store but no business. He lived a good life, but there didn't seem to be a source of income. The only explanation he ever gave was to say that his mother had money for him. I believe he was taking money from your parents and, like you said one time, returning none."

"I believe that is what happened."

She heard the caution in his voice. "It was a terrible shock to realize you were the stepbrother I sought."

"I well imagine it was." Still not an ounce of understanding that she could tell.

"For so long I had blamed his stepbrother for Frank's death. It was easier than blaming myself."

He caught her arms. "You are not to blame."

"I know that, but neither are you or the stepbrother I imagined." She struggled to speak the next words but she had to. It was the only way to put this business behind her. "No one is to blame for Frank's choices. They belong to him alone."

"Exactly."

"My choices are also mine alone."

He tensed.

"And I choose to willingly be your wife and a mother to Anna."

It took a moment for her words to register, but she knew the moment he did. In fact the whole camp did. He let out a whoop that set the dog to barking and the mules to braying. He wrapped his arms around her.

"That is the best news ever." He leaned back so he could look into her face.

She studied him, his face angular in the light from the campfire. She could not see his eyes well enough to read his feelings. Perhaps his whoop said it all, but she longed for words. "I'm holding you to the promise you gave me." She quoted the words that were in the front of the poetry book.

He tipped his forehead to hers. "All my adult life I have wanted someone who would be loyal to me. Or at least that's how I chose to view it. But I want more. So much more. I want a love that does not change with circumstances. A love that is faithful through good times and bad." His voice deepened. "That's what I am giving you. I'm giving you my heart with no strings attached."

"It's the best gift I could ask for. I, too, give you my heart with no strings attached."

"Judith Trapper, my wife, I love you."

She whooped. The dog barked. The mules brayed. She didn't care. She'd wondered if he would ever say those three little words that made all the difference.

"Gil Trapper, my husband, I love you."

He didn't whoop again. He laughed then caught her lips in a claiming, promising kiss. She held him close, her hands at his back, pressing him close. This was the beginning of their life of love and she meant to enjoy every heartbeat of it and brand it forever on her memory.

She knew it must be her imagination, but it seemed the sky filled with light.

"It's a comet," he said and they stared heavenward as falling star after falling star streaked across the sky.

"Could we ask for a better blessing on our love?" she asked.

EPILOGUE

For two days, Judith worked long and hard on the sampler she made wanting to finish it as quickly as possible and give it to Gil as a wedding present. A visible sign of their commitment to each other.

She finished it before they stopped for supper and she folded it into her pocket. Once they reached their new home, she would press it and frame it.

Donna Grace asked why she smiled as they made supper together.

"I have a surprise for Gil," Judith answered.

Donna Grace nodded, her smile full of sweetness as if she remembered special things she and Luke had shared.

Judith's brothers and the ladies of the group had noticed the change in Judith's and Gil's relationship and had conspired together to make a special evening for Judith and Gil. They would take care of Anna while Judith and Gil had an evening to themselves.

Gil had taken the tent a hundred feet from the circled wagons into the shelter of some trees. When Judith let it be known she feared raiders, her brothers informed her their little camp would be well guarded.

Already Gil had a campfire burning brightly and Judith's heart picked up pace. She prepared plates of food for each of them and started across the grass. Gil saw her and trotted over to help her.

Judith felt unaccustomedly shy. They'd been married three weeks, had spent seven—almost eight days—in isolation, but this was the first time they had been alone as man and wife.

He had placed a log close to the fire and they sat side by side as they ate supper.

As soon as they finished, she said, "I have a gift for you." She pulled out the sampler she'd labored over, each stitch sewn with love.

She'd made a house with flowers at every window and a swing on the porch. A river flowed nearby. Children played by the house under the branches of a blossom-laden tree. On the door, she'd stitched the word *joy*. As a title, she written *happiness and contentment*.

He took it. "Judith, this is beautiful." He cleared his throat. "I have nothing for you."

She touched the picture. "You gave me the promise this picture portrays." She repeated the words he had spoken to her not so long ago. "They are penned in the flyleaf of a poetry book. But most of all, they are here."

She touched her chest. "In my heart." Her throat tightened, but she went on. "You are the best gift I could ask for."

"Things might not be easy in the future."

She smiled. "I don't care so long as we face the future together. It is not an easy life I want. It's to share with you whatever God sends, be it trials and tribulations or an overabundance of good things."

He folded the bit of cloth and tucked it carefully into his pocket. Then he took her in his arms and they kissed.

Their future promised to be one full of joy and contentment.

ALSO BY LINDA FORD

Contemporary Romance

Montana Skies series

Cry of My Heart

Forever in My Heart

Everlasting Love

Inheritance of Love

Historical Romance

Dakota Brides series

Temporary Bride

Abandoned Bride

Second-Chance Bride

Reluctant Bride

War Brides series

Lizzie

Maryelle

Irene

Grace

Wild Rose Country

Crane's Bride

Hannah's Dream

Chastity's Angel

Cowboy Bodyguard